RUSHED: CHRISTOPHER

A "THE FOUR" NOVELLA

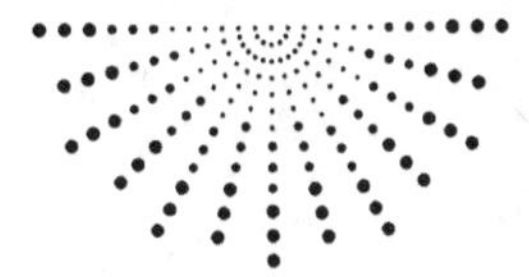

SLOANE KENNEDY

AUTHOR NOTE

While this novella is linked to my "The Four" series, it can be read as a stand-alone story.

TRIGGER WARNING NOTE

Trigger warnings for this book are located on the next page. For those who do not want any kind of "spoilers" that the warning may reveal, skip the next page.

TRIGGER WARNING

Includes references to sexual assault of a minor, HIV/AIDS and discussion of HIV/AIDS stigma.

PROLOGUE

CHRISTOPHER

☦4

I knew we were in trouble from the second the beefy-looking bouncer smiled at us and waved us past without asking for ID. If that fact alone hadn't been enough to assure me that this was a really, really bad idea, the huge man clinched it by settling a knowing grin (and not the good kind) on us and adding, "Have fun, boys. The guys are just going to eat you up."

Say something, Christopher! Do something!

It was my own voice I was hearing in my head, and it had been screaming those same words into every brain cell since I could remember. But just like all the other times, I kept my mouth shut and followed my best friend and quasi-cousin, Gio, into the club.

The air inside was thick with the stench of sweat, sex, and weed, much like the smell of the house I'd spent the first fourteen years of my life growing up in. Just like back then, it made me sick to my stomach. So did the all-too-familiar sight of people fucking in plain sight. That had been a staple in my childhood home too, just like all the needles and glass pipes that had been lying on every usable surface in every room of the house.

Except my room.

I'd always been safe in my room, lost in a book so I wouldn't have to hear any of what had been happening on the other side of that door. My uncle Micah had always made sure he was between me and whatever dangers lurked outside my precious stories and that weak, worn wooden door.

No matter what it cost him.

My body jerked when I saw two guys fucking up against the wall. The bigger guy had the smaller one pressed face-first against the rough-looking surface. My vision dimmed as a wave of unbearable heat flashed through me followed by an equally painful, bitter cold that made my veins feel like ice.

I could feel the hot breath on the back of my neck as the stench of cologne wafted all around me.

So sweet, little one. Nice and quiet just like my special boy was. Do you want to be my special boy just like your uncle Micah was?

A bright flash of light thankfully brought me back to the present and saved me from what could have been the panic attack from hell, but the relief was short-lived as I realized we were in the main part of the club and the interior was a brighter, louder, more crowded version of the hallway.

I wanted to turn tail and run. I wanted to beg Gio to forget his mission to confront the man he'd long ago lost his heart to. But my best friend needed closure, and there was no way I could leave him alone in a place like this.

But even as I vowed that this time I *wasn't* going to be the pathetic coward that I was, my mind was screaming at me that this was all wrong. I could feel the eyes on me. Even though Gio was drop-dead gorgeous with his pale hair and fair features whereas I wouldn't stand out in a crowd even if I was on fire, I knew that in this terrible, dangerous place, we were the same in one chilling way.

We were both prey.

"Gio, we should go," I managed to choke out. My skin itched, and I couldn't breathe. My body felt like it weighed a thousand pounds instead of the whole hundred pounds soaking wet that it actually did.

"Yeah," Gio responded unexpectedly. The mere fact that he was agreeing with me was proof that we were way in over our heads. I tried to take in a deep breath, but all I got was lungs full of smoke.

I was practically glued to Gio's side as we turned and began making our way back the way we'd come, but we didn't make it more than a couple of steps before three behemoths stepped into our path. Gio stuck his arm toward me, and coward that I was, I took his hand and let him place me at his back so that he alone was facing what I knew in my gut was a very real threat.

I managed to catch a few of the words the biggest of the men said to Gio, but my addled brain couldn't make sense of them. I could only cling to Gio's jacket and keep my eyes down in the hopes that the move would somehow miraculously make me invisible.

It didn't.

Before I knew it, heavy fingers were wrapping around my fore-arm, a feat I couldn't make sense of since I'd been using Gio as a shield. But the proof was biting into my skin, and I couldn't help but let out a little squeak of pain and fear. I could feel my brain shutting down in an effort to protect itself from what was coming. I'd seen all the times my uncle had been grabbed in the same way and even though I'd pretended as hard as I could that everything was okay, I'd known what was happening behind the closed door of the room he'd been taken into.

"Hey, leave him alone," Gio yelled as he shoved the guy holding me away.

Even though the pain on my forearm was gone, I could still feel the weight of the man's hand as strongly as if he still had a hold of me.

Run! Get help!

The internal command fell on deaf ears, and I could only stand mutely as one of the guys grabbed Gio from behind and dragged him backward. I allowed myself to drift to that quiet little spot in my head where the scene that was playing out before me was nothing more than words on a page. Reality fell away as I waited for the hero to intercede like he did in all of my books.

It didn't matter how much the characters despised each other in any one of the hundreds of romance novels I'd read over the years... the rescue always came. The hero would show up just in time...

My safe space fell away as someone grabbed me from behind. I couldn't tell if it was the same guy from before, but it didn't really matter. With the way Gio was struggling and the lack of response from any of the dozens of club patrons nearby, I knew what was about to happen.

"Gio?" I heard myself call out. I needed him to tell me what to do. I needed him to tell me because the ugly truth was hitting me like a ton of bricks.

There would be no hero. There would be no rescue.

The man holding me began forcing me to walk straight toward a single curtained doorway. It was all I could do not to break down in tears. My uncle Micah would have automatically known what to do, and his husband, Con, well, he'd have neutralized the situation in a second flat. But I wasn't an MMA fighter like Con, and for some reason, I couldn't remember even one of the self-defense moves he'd taught me over the years.

Just before we reached the curtain, I heard a scuffle behind me but couldn't see anything.

For about three seconds.

Then, just like that, I heard the guy holding me scream in pain, and then his hands were gone.

I was free.

Still, I was slow to turn around in case it was a trick.

"Christopher, run!" Gio called.

I spun around to see Gio struggling with one of the three attackers. The other two were focused on their injuries—injuries Gio had apparently inflicted on them.

The third guy slammed his fist into the side of Gio's head, and just like that, Gio went limp. My mind raced as I tried to figure out how to save both of us. As I scanned our surroundings while the men regrouped, I saw it.

Salvation.

I lunged for the fire alarm on the wall next to the curtained doorway, but strong fingers closed around my wrist before I could pull the lever. I wanted to cry in frustration at the loss. I was slammed hard against a chest and then shoved forward through the curtain. I tried looking over my shoulder for Gio, but the man holding me gave me a hard jerk and then yanked me closer.

"You're going to pay for that, you little bitch," the man growled into my ear.

I ignored the chill that ran up my spine and called, "Gio!" The move earned me a hard yank on my hair, and meaty fingers closed around my throat.

"It's always the quiet ones that put up the best fight," the guy murmured as he ran his nose along my neck and up to my ear.

The tears I'd been desperately trying to fight off began to fall. I heard the men exchange crude remarks, and then I was dragged farther down the darkened hallway. I was only released long enough to be shoved through an open doorway. I desperately tried to get back to the quiet place in my head where my white knight had just gallantly saved me and was declaring his love for me, but the escape eluded me as easily as any hope for a physical one.

I didn't have enough mental capacity to take in much about the room other than the single mattress in the center that didn't have so much as even a sheet on it.

"Get on the bed, princess."

I knew he wanted me to protest or fight him in some way, but I also knew what would happen if I did. And the reality was that I couldn't let him push me against the wall.

So sweet, little one. Do you want to be my special boy...?

I moved stiffly to the bed.

"Get on your stomach."

I hated myself for doing what he said. I couldn't even make my mouth spit out the one little word that was screaming on a loop in my head.

No!

I tried to hold my breath as I lay down across the bed, but the stench of stale sweat and sex assailed my nose anyway. I only had seconds to think about it because a moment later, a heavy weight sank down on me, pinning me to the mattress from head to toe. The man smelled like cigar smoke and whiskey. I nearly gagged when his breath washed over me as he nuzzled the side of my face.

"Now show me all the fight you've got inside, princess."

I closed my eyes, no longer able to control the tears. They fell silently down my cheeks. The asshole had to have felt them. The tears and the violent shaking of my entire body became completely uncontrollable when I realized I might not be able to escape to my safe space in my head at all.

"Please," I whispered.

The guy ground his dick against my ass. "Begging works too," he said snidely, and then his hand was between our bodies and he was lowering his zipper. "Turn over, princess. Let's put that pretty little mouth of yours to use."

I shook my head slowly but didn't try to stop him from turning me over. If I just kept my eyes closed, it wouldn't be real. None of it would be real.

That was my last thought before I heard a crashing sound in the room next to the one we were in. My eyes flew open just in time to see the guy over me looking worriedly at the wall that separated our rooms.

An instant later, the door to our room was kicked in. I tried to process what was happening, but all I could make sense of was that the heavy weight was gone as were the cruel fingers. I curled myself into a ball and squeezed my eyes closed even tighter in the hopes of finally reaching the quiet place.

Miraculously, I managed it because within a minute or so, I no longer heard the sound of flesh striking flesh or grunts of pain.

It was quiet.

So blessedly quiet.

Unfortunately, it didn't last.

"Christopher?"

I didn't recognize the voice. It wasn't the same guy from before, but that didn't mean anything in this hellhole. I shook my head but not in response to his probing of my name.

"Please, don't." I buried my face in the disgusting bed and sought out the pages of one of my favorite books.

"Christopher, my name is Rush. I work with King."

"King?"

It was the only word in his statement that made sense in my addled brain.

"Yeah, King. He's in the next room with Gio, and when you're ready, I'll take you over there."

King was here? He was with Gio?

Reality returned like a punch to the gut. I jerked upright, striking a solid form in the process. Strong fingers closed around my upper arms, but unlike the ones before, they were gentle. Gone was the stench of alcohol and cigars, and in its place was the muted crispness of one of my favorite aftershaves.

My hands were stuck between my body and what proved to be a very broad chest.

"Are you hurt?" the man—Rush... he'd said his name was Rush— asked as his hands swept up and down my forearms. Some of the chill began to leach from my system as Rush's body heat began to envelop me.

I shook my head and willed myself not to cry like I wanted.

"Gio," I croaked. "I need to see if…"

"He's okay, Christopher. We got to you in time," Rush said with unfound certainty. Then, strangely enough, he pulled me forward into his arms, dropped his head on top of mine, and whispered, "We got to you in time."

This time, his voice held not only certainty but relief as well. I felt his body shudder slightly against mine, as if he were letting out a relieved breath.

Had he and King been worried about *not* reaching us in time? The reminder of what would have happened if they hadn't had me wanting to throw up then and there.

Instead, I wrapped my arms tightly around Rush's waist. He

returned the embrace with a level of fervor that had nothing to do with intimacy and everything to do with comfort. I couldn't say how long we stood there like that for, but it likely wasn't long given the situation. I loosened my hold on Rush and stepped back a little. I was both glad and disappointed when he let me go.

"Thank—" I began as I lifted my eyes to Rush's face. As I quickly took in his gorgeous features, I stumbled over the rest of what I'd been trying to say. "Thank you, Rush."

I quickly dropped my eyes because Rush's dark eyes were just too damn intense. I knew they couldn't be black, but they were such a deep shade of brown that they may as well have been.

I fully expected the man who had at least six inches and seventy-five pounds on me to lead me from the room, but he surprised me when his gentle fingers brushed my chin and then urged my face up. Since he was holding me in the position, I allowed myself to drink my fill of him. Tan skin, black hair that was just a bit unruly, and dark brows framing eyes that I just knew in my gut would only be readable if the man behind them allowed it.

Like he was doing now.

I couldn't really make sense of what I was seeing. Concern, yes, but it went deeper than that. He was studying me like… like he knew me or something, yet I'd never met the man in my life.

The show of what I could only call emotion rattled me, and I found myself dropping my eyes a bit.

They landed on his mouth.

His really pretty mouth that was surrounded by just a bit of scruff that, like his hair, was dark.

Despite Rush's hold on my chin, when I dropped my eyes even more, they unfortunately landed on the guy who'd dragged me into the room. I automatically jumped back to put some distance between us, but Rush easily caught me and said, "He's out, Christopher. And he's not coming to anytime soon, I promise you."

I felt sick to my stomach at the sight of the man but not because his face looked like hamburger. The truth about what the man would have done to me had Rush not shown up was sinking in. I supposed that even as he'd been about to force me to perform some sex act on him, somewhere deep inside I'd believed my knight in shining armor would come.

And he had.

That was twice now.

Micah had saved me when I'd been fourteen, and Rush had saved me now. Would luck strike a third time? If I was out on a date with some guy and he got too forward, would there be someone to stop him? What if some random guy grabbed me off the street as I was walking on the sidewalk and stuck a gun in my gut while demanding all my money?

No… no, I wouldn't be able to stop him. Not him and not Date Guy. I wasn't brave enough. Tonight had been proof of that.

If I'd helped Gio when he'd fought back… if I'd tried just a little harder to reach that fire alarm…

"Christopher?"

Rush's voice brought me back to the present. Funnily enough, my eyes automatically went to his hands. They were heavily bruised and covered in blood that looked like it had been wiped off as best as it could be.

"Christopher?"

I wanted to cry because Rush's voice was even gentler now, and there was no missing the pity in it.

I nodded and stepped forward. I was grateful that Rush kept his body between mine and my attacker's.

As we left the room, there were a few gawkers in various states of undress outside both my door and the door of the room Gio had been taken into. I froze in place because I didn't want any one of those people to touch me. Even by accident.

"Whoa, I've got you," Rush said softly, his big body nearly brushing mine from behind. He put an arm protectively around my chest while his upper body pressed against my back as he urged me forward. I didn't feel trapped or restrained in any kind of way.

I felt… *safe.*

But I knew it was all temporary. I could call Rush my knight in shining armor or my hero or whatever, but once this hellish night was over, he'd be gone.

A cold, ugly truth settled over me. It was something my uncle King had even tried to warn me about it.

Life wasn't a romance novel. Bad things happened, and when they did, there wasn't always someone there to stop it.

I'd gotten lucky twice.

There wouldn't be a third. I knew that in my gut.

Which left only one thing to do…

CHAPTER ONE

RUSH

+4

"Here."

I actually let out a little grunt when King shoved a huge and really fucking heavy box into my arms. On the side of the box was the word *books* written out in black marker.

"What the fuck?" I began and then saw King lift another box, which he unceremoniously dropped on top of the one I was already holding. "Dude," I said as my muscles began to feel the strain. "I thought we were going for a beer."

"We are," my boss responded even as he got yet another box of books out of the back of his truck. Thankfully, he held on to that one himself and used one arm to lift the tailgate. "Just a little side trip," he added. The man seemed uncharacteristically annoyed but not angry.

I'd seen King angry.

It wasn't a pretty sight.

Fortunately, I'd never been on his bad side, and in our line of work, anger pretty much came with the territory. But saving kids from sex trafficking rings meant you had to have a certain kind of cool anger.

Controlled anger.

And a strong gut.

I'd already had the first by the time I'd enlisted in the army, and it hadn't taken long to develop the second. Having to watch the heads of men and even women who may or may not be carrying a bomb under their clothing explode from a hail of bullets taught a man how to not lose the contents of his stomach every five minutes.

I stayed silent as I followed King up the steps of a small Cape Cod–style house in the suburbs north of Seattle. Having only recently set down roots in the city myself, I had yet to learn what was what when it came to the Emerald City, but I was liking everything I saw. The lush greenery, epic mountain views, sapphire waters of Puget Sound, and even the somewhat seemingly endless rain made it a little easier to leave the past behind.

Despite the boxes, I managed to take in a few things about the house. For one, it sat on a nice sizeable corner lot and had a view of the sound as well as the towering mountains of the Olympic Peninsula. Even though it seemed to be in a good neighborhood that sported clean streets, neatly maintained yards, and kids riding their bikes down the block or shooting hoops in their driveways, the house I was getting glimpses of was significantly lacking in the TLC department. The yard was overgrown, as were the flower beds. The white trim was in sad need of a new coat of paint while the siding was screaming for a good power washing. My fingers practically itched to get to work on the poor little neglected house. I found myself annoyed at the owner for letting the place go to hell.

I tamped the emotion down and focused on making it up the single porch step that led to the front door. Even though there was a doorbell, King slammed his fist against the door several times. I managed to rest my boxes on the porch's railing. King's irritation had me on alert. No way was this thing about just dropping off some boxes to whoever lived here.

"King, what's the plan?" I asked.

"Tough love, that's the plan," King said solemnly as he knocked again, though more softly this time.

I didn't hear any approaching footsteps from the other side of the door, but after several beats, someone called out, "Who's there?"

"It's King. Open up." King responded. His voice was firm but not harsh.

It should have only taken a second to open the door, but as one lock after another was worked open, it took closer to a minute. Whoever was on the other side of that door clearly had some safety concerns.

I settled my ass against the rail, even as I used one hand to keep the boxes in place. I had a full view of the doorway, so I recognized him instantly. Long before he timidly stepped into the doorway and peeked his head out, not to look at his uncle but to scan the street and our surroundings.

Christopher.

The young man I'd saved from what would have been a brutal assault.

My stomach flipped as I took in his features. Instead of filling out like I'd assumed he would when I'd met the skinny teenager, the now twenty-two-year-old looked even thinner.

And haggard.

So fucking haggard.

Like he'd been in a war zone.

Dark smudges stained the skin under his almost sunken-looking eyes. His clothes were loose and too big for him. Or more likely, they'd fit him at some point when he'd been at a healthy weight.

When Christopher's eyes fell on me, he instantly stepped back into the house a few feet and used the door as a shield. I glanced at King and saw a horrified expression cross his features before he managed to mask it.

"Um, hi," Christopher said quietly. He dropped his eyes slightly, like he knew what his uncle was seeing and was waiting to be called out on it.

"Hey, kiddo," King said as he straightened and walked into the house. I remained where I was but had enough of a view to see King put the box down on the floor before he wrapped his arms around

Christopher. I couldn't hear what he said to the young man, but what-ever it was, Christopher didn't seem to react to it.

I couldn't make sense of it.

The young man was nothing like the teenager I'd helped four years earlier. Yes, that Christopher had been solemn and quiet and right-fully slow. But he'd still been... *alive*. The young man before me who seemed to struggle to return his uncle's embrace was just a shell.

"You remember Rush?" King said to Christopher as he released him and then motioned in my direction.

Christopher's eyes on me had my stomach knotting up. Yes, I'd helped him four years ago, but I was also a reminder of what had happened to him that night. It shouldn't have mattered either way, but it did.

It really did.

I wanted him to be okay with me. I wanted to know that I wasn't someone he had to fear. Even worse, I was overcome with the urge to pull him into my arms like I had that night and tell him the words I hadn't been able to utter at the time because I'd been too overcome with the relief of knowing I'd gotten to him in time.

I've got you.

From the moment I'd touched Christopher, I'd felt the weight of possessiveness fall over me like a shroud. It wasn't something I'd ever felt with any of the men or women I'd dated over the years. Even the few long-term relationships I'd had hadn't merited that kind of reaction.

Thankfully, time and distance had forced me to get past the strange emotions. Christopher had returned home, and I'd gone back to work, and we hadn't crossed paths again.

Until now.

And just like that, that mantel was back. I wanted answers. I wanted to fix whatever had broken inside of the young man in the time since I'd last seen him. But it wasn't just the need to protect... there was something else there too.

Something I'd been ashamed to mentally admit to four years ago.

I'd been painfully attracted to Christopher. It hadn't mattered that he was trying to deal with nearly being sexually assaulted. It hadn't mattered that he was young and clearly innocent. It hadn't even mattered that he was technically my boss's nephew.

I'd wanted him… badly.

And with the way my heart began racing and my dick began filling, it appeared I still did.

"I can go wait in the car," I offered when Christopher's eyes met mine and he didn't say anything.

The young man didn't instantly respond. His eyes scanned me from head to toe, but there was nothing intimate in the move. It seemed more like he was looking for danger. He finally shook his head and said, "No, I'm sorry. Please, come in, Rush."

I gave him a second to change his mind before straightening and grabbing the boxes. As soon as I walked past him, Christopher shut the door and began engaging one lock after another. I followed King, who'd picked up his own box to the kitchen. By the time Christopher joined us, all three boxes were sitting on the table.

"Figured now that you've got your own place, you'd want these back," King said as he patted one of the boxes. Christopher finally seemed to notice the writing on the outside of the boxes and instantly paled.

Instead of just leaving things as they were, King opened one of the boxes. With the movement of every flap of the cardboard, Christopher grew more and more tense.

I knew King could tell what he was doing was bothering Christopher, but it didn't stop him.

Tough love.

That's what King had called it.

King opened the box to reveal dozens upon dozens of paperback books. I recognized them instantly because I'd had more than one girlfriend who'd read the very same kind of books. They were romance novels. I couldn't be sure that all of the books in the box were the same or if the other two boxes also had romances in them, but one thing was clear when I glanced at Christopher.

He loved them.

Stop. Period. End of sentence.

He absolutely loved them.

But instead of reaching for one or expressing his thanks, Christopher wrapped his skinny arms around his body and took several steps back. His eyes grew haunted as he looked at the books, and then, just like that, the love was gone, replaced by sheer contempt.

What the fuck?

"This one's your favorite, right?" King said as he grabbed one of the books and began flipping through it. "Gio got it on his Kindle, and now he's hooked on the whole series," King continued. "He's not the only one," he added with a small smile.

It was painful to watch my friend try and draw his nephew out. King had told me about the events of Christopher's childhood and how their own bond had been established. Christopher's real uncle, Micah, had raised his nephew pretty much single-handedly in an abusive household. Thankfully, Christopher had escaped the worst of the violence, but only because his uncle had taken it all upon himself. Christopher hadn't been left unscathed though. A violent encounter in the house had led to Christopher and his younger sister fleeing as Micah had fended off the attacker. Fortunately, King's brother, Con, had had a history with Micah and had been outside the house, along with King, in his car. As Con had gone to help Micah, King had followed the children.

I knew the version of events I'd been told nowhere near covered the horror of it, but one thing was clear. Whatever had happened between Christopher and King that night had bonded them as uncle and nephew, not by blood but of the heart. If King was playing hardball with Christopher, things had to be pretty bad.

"I'm sorry you brought them all the way over here, but I told Gio to just throw them away if he didn't want them," Christopher murmured. If I hadn't been looking at him, I might have believed in his dispassionate statement, but the way the young man looked at the books when he mentioned throwing them away was actually painful.

King sighed, seemingly unsurprised by the response. "Talk to me,

Christopher…" my boss said so softly I almost didn't hear him. King was the hardest man I knew, so for him to ask the young man like that… well, it just fucking sucked.

As much as I wanted to hear what Christopher's response was, I'd already been privy to far too much, so I eased out of the kitchen in the hopes of not drawing attention to myself.

Mission *not* accomplished.

One second, I was turning around and heading for the door; the next, I was doing some not-so-fancy footwork to avoid a kitten that had appeared out of nowhere. Unfortunately, my forward momentum made it impossible to maintain my balance, and I pitched forward. I somehow managed to stay on my feet, but it wasn't pretty as I stepped forward in an almost slow-motion running fashion while trying to regain my equilibrium. Inopportunely, the tiny orange ball of fur decided to escape in the same direction and once again ran straight in front of me. Knowing that even just the weight of my foot could crush a part of the kitten's body, I instinctively reached down even as I began falling. I managed to scoop up the freaked feline and cuddled him to my chest as best as I could as I twisted my body so my back would take the brunt of the fall.

When it was all over, I was sprawled out on my back on the very hard floor with many, many mini razor-like claws embedded in my chest. To make matters worse, several pieces of what had once been some kind of side table were scattered around and beneath me, proving my pride and the freaked-out ball of fur hanging onto my chest hadn't been the only victims of my clumsiness. The glass that was near my hip indicated there'd been at least one other victim of the melee. From the size of the pieces, I guessed I'd managed to take down a lamp, shattering the bulb in the process.

"Oh God," I heard someone cry. Definitely not King, so that left Christopher. My body hurt like a son of a bitch as I shifted my weight a bit before detaching the kitten from my chest. The pitiful little thing was making soft mewling sounds but otherwise seemed to be okay. Before I could sit up, Christopher was at my side.

"Careful, there's glass," I said as I took in Christopher's bare feet. Instead of him risking cutting himself by getting too close to me, I lifted the kitten toward him as best as I could. Predictably, he snatched the little thing up and hugged it to his chest. I dropped my head back down as I took stock of my injuries, which I knew were nowhere near as severe as the hit to my pride.

"You okay?" I heard King ask. I could hear the humor in his voice and knew I wouldn't be hearing the end of this for a long while. I had my eyes closed, but I could already sense his presence standing above me, probably near my feet.

I opened my mouth to tell him to fuck off but then suddenly Christopher was saying, "Here, take him." Confused by the statement, I opened my eyes only to find Christopher in the process of gently handing over the kitten to King, and then he was dropping to his knees next to me. I managed to swipe my hand across the floor to clear away most of the glass before Christopher's body came in contact with it.

"What hurts?" Christopher asked as he took my hand in his. Despite the laughable situation, there was nothing funny about the sparks of energy that danced up my arm as Christopher's slim fingers came into contact with my skin. The young man's worried emerald eyes scanned my body.

It felt like he was doing it with his fingers. At least, that was the way my body was reacting to the whole thing. God, if he *did* start putting his hands on me...

"I'm good," I said as I tried to sit up. Christopher's surprisingly strong hands closed over my shoulders, stopping me from sitting up all the way.

"No, give it a minute. You hit your head. You're bleeding."

At most, the shoulder that had taken the brunt of the fall was a bit sore, so if there was any bleeding, the wound was paltry at best. I was about to tell Christopher pretty much exactly that when he leaned forward until his mouth was only half a dozen inches from mine. I doubted he even noticed the proximity because his eyes were focused on my temple. I was forced to brace myself on my elbows to maintain the position since the young man seemingly wasn't going to let me sit up anytime soon, and I didn't want to be flat on my back with him hovering over me. *That* would have put way too many images in my head.

Of course, having Christopher's supple lips right *there* wasn't ideal either. I was very close to telling him one kiss would make everything better.

"Does your neck or back hurt?" Christopher asked.

I was about to give him the stock answer that I was fine when he chose to look me in the eye again.

And something shifted inside of me.

The air between us became filled with tension, though neither of us moved. Not forward, not backward.

It would be so easy. A well-placed hand at the base of his neck, a few inches of leaning in…

Christopher sucked in a breath as he suddenly seemed to realize the position we were in… that *he* was in. I fully expected him to jerk back or at least turn his head to break the contact, but to my surprise, he leaned in a little more. His fingers were still at my temple, but instead of exploring whatever injury was there, his thumb began rhythmically stroking back and forth while his palm covered the side of my face.

Holding me in place.

Not that I needed to be held. I had no intention of going anywhere.

It was the sound of the kitten crying that broke through the charged moment. Christopher lurched back so fast that I ended up putting my arm around his waist to keep him from scrambling away and cutting his feet on the little bit of glass that was still near us.

"You should, um, lay down on the couch, and I'll… I'll get some bandages for that cut," Christopher said nervously. His eyes shifted to my arm that was still keeping him immobile. I reluctantly released him.

"I'm fine, really, Christopher. It'd take at least a coffee table and three floor lamps to take me out," I joked.

The small smile that drifted across Christopher's mouth was like watching the sun break through the clouds.

"I'll be right back," he said shyly, and then he was climbing to his feet. He stepped over my body, gracefully navigating the glass and wood, and then hurried up the stairs that I assumed led to his bedroom.

My eyes were still on his pert ass when I heard the crunching of glass.

Fuck.

I pushed myself to a sitting position, avoiding King's eyes as long as possible. If the man had seen me ogling his nephew's ass... well, then I really would be facing a world of hurt.

"Snipers, IEDs, suicide bombings, only to finally be taken down by three pounds of cuteness," my boss said as he held out his hand. I grabbed it and let him pull me to my feet.

"Shut up," I growled because I had nothing better to say. I glanced over my shoulder at the damage my clumsiness had caused. The table was beyond repair, but thankfully, the lamp hadn't been damaged aside from the broken bulb. "Tell me that wasn't some kind of family heirloom or something," I said.

I looked around the house to try and figure out from the other furnishings if they were newer or if they had any kind of antique flair to them. That was when I noticed the wall between the kitchen and the dining room was being torn down.

Or someone was *trying* to tear it down. There were a few small holes here and there but not placed strategically enough to make it easier to bring the wall down in large pieces.

"Here," King said as he suddenly shoved the kitten into my arms. "He's coming."

"What?" I asked stupidly. I could hear footsteps overhead, but what did that matter?

I had my answer when King said, "Do this for me, and I'll explain later."

I opened my mouth to ask what the hell he was talking about when he suddenly grabbed my free arm and practically dragged me to the couch. He shoved me unceremoniously down onto it just as footsteps began coming down the steps. King pulled his phone out and put it to his ear without even dialing. Just as Christopher appeared, King said, "Yeah, Gio, I'm on my way."

I was about to ask King what the fuck he was doing when Christopher worriedly asked, "Is Gio okay?"

"Oh yeah, he's fine," King explained. "Faucet's busted. Water's spraying all over the place." Barely pausing, King looked at me and said, "Sorry, buddy, gotta cancel on dinner tonight. Hopefully you can scrounge something up on your own." As he talked, King started walking toward the front door. "Maybe try that deli next to your hotel. They might have some cold sandwiches or something."

Was he seriously not only intentionally leaving me alone with Christopher but trying to angle a dinner invitation for me by implying I had no way to get a hot meal for myself? What the fuck was he up to? And didn't he know that two could play the game?

"Faucet's broken?" I said, catching King before he could make his escape.

"Uh, yeah."

"So water's spraying all over the kitchen. Flooding it, I suppose," I observed as I carefully settled the kitten on my lap. Christopher stood in silence, his head moving back and forth like he was watching a tennis game.

"Yeah, that's right. A lot of potential for water damage," King said, his hand on the knob of the now open door.

"Oh, that's bad," I agreed. "But you *did* tell him to just turn the water off beneath the sink, right?"

King gave me a dark look promising retribution and then muttered something he purposefully kept too soft for us to hear as he closed the door behind him.

There was a pregnant pause as Christopher and I seemed to come to the same realization at the same time.

It was just me and him.

"I really should get going," I said, but as I began to stand, Christopher hurried to my side and urged me to sit again by putting his hand on my shoulder. Despite not having known him well four years ago, I felt like I was being given a glimpse into the old Christopher.

The one I hadn't had enough time to get to know.

I reminded myself that I wasn't supposed to get to know the young man. Not only was there more than ten years between us, but his normally overprotective uncle also happened to be the man who signed my paychecks.

"Let me just clean this up," Christopher said as he motioned to the cut on my head. "I want to make sure there's no glass in it," he added. Instead of just the couple of bandages I was expecting to see him holding, he had what looked like a tackle box in his hand.

Rather than sitting next to me on the couch, he pulled an ottoman forward and used that, putting us face-to-face. Our eyes met briefly, but Christopher quickly dropped his eyes. I dropped my own and studied the kitten, who had calmed considerably and was trying to stand on my thigh. The poor thing wobbled considerably as it began walking across my lap.

"Oh, fuck, Christopher," I whispered as I realized I'd ended up hurting the kitten somehow after all.

"He's okay, Rush," Christopher said at the same time that one of his hands covered mine where it was resting on my knee. The combination of his touch and the use of my name had me looking up. Christopher paused as that weird energy thing happened between us again. I knew exactly what it was, but I wasn't sure Christopher did. He eased his hand back once again and dropped his eyes. When he'd first sat down, he hadn't seemed nervous or stressed, but something had changed.

"He, um, he's got a neurological disorder," Christopher said as he carefully reached one hand out and petted the little cat. "The vet said he probably got injured when he was just a baby. He's not in any pain… he just can't react as quickly to things, and obviously his balance is off."

I looked down at the cat and tried very hard to ignore Christopher's hand as it stroked over the cat, which was now starting to settle down for a nap.

In my lap.

Precariously close to the goods.

"If you hadn't grabbed him like that when you fell..." Christopher whispered. He couldn't finish the sentence, and there was no missing the way his eyes watered.

"What's his name?" I asked, more to give Christopher a chance to recover from the emotions the potential loss of or injury to his pet had brought out.

"Pip."

I smiled as I took in the tiny cat's fragile body.

"I loved her against reason, against promise, against peace, against hope, against happiness—" I began.

"—against all discouragement that could be," Christopher finished. He paused as he seemed to digest the beauty of the sentence and then asked, "How did you know I named him after Pip in *Great Expectations?*"

I nodded at several boxes in the corner of the living room next to an empty bookshelf. Like the ones King and I had carried into the house, they were sealed up and had the word *books* written on them.

"You clearly like to read, so I took a chance," I said.

"It's one of my favorites," Christopher acknowledged.

I told myself to keep my mouth shut because we seemed to be in a good place. But the need to know was too great. "And the ones in the kitchen?" I asked.

Christopher stopped petting the cat and started to look in that direction before stopping abruptly and reaching for the weird tackle box thing.

"Fairy tales. Nothing more," he muttered coldly.

He flipped open the box, which revealed a whole host of medical supplies.

"What's wrong with fairy tales?" I asked carefully.

"Nothing," Christopher responded as he began rifling through the box. "Unless you're too foolish to realize they're all lies. And by the time you do…"

When he didn't continue, I said, "And by the time you do?"

Christopher stilled for several long beats. If I hadn't been watching him carefully, I would have missed the slight tremor in his hand as his fingers hovered over something in the box.

"Then it's already too late."

CHAPTER TWO

CHRISTOPHER

☥4

I wanted to smack myself as soon as the words were out. I hadn't meant to say any of that. I hadn't meant to say anything *at all*, but something about the man before me was making it nearly impossible to hold my tongue.

Just patch him up and get him out.

The internal voice was mine, but the words weren't.

Not really.

It wasn't something I could easily explain, even to myself. It was like my mind was warring with itself. New Christopher versus old. Cynical, bitter Christopher versus shy, quiet Christopher.

The battle usually only raged when I was around my family, but for some reason, the dual sides decided Rush fell into that category of wishing I could go back to the past.

To before I'd let my life become the mess that it was.

I sighed and forced myself to focus on the task at hand. But even as I began automatically pulling the supplies I'd need out of the box, I couldn't help but shoot glances at Rush.

He looked much like he had four years earlier with the only noticeable difference being that there was now a hint of silver in both his hair and the scruff that did nothing to diminish the fullness of his lips.

There was also one other difference between now and the last time we'd met.

I wanted him.

Badly.

Considering the circumstances of how we'd met four years ago, being attracted to the man hadn't even been on my radar at the time.

But now?

I wanted to kill my uncle. Not only had he brought the gorgeous Rush into my house, but he'd left me alone with him.

And I'd let King do it.

I knew for a fact that my best friend knew how to turn the water beneath a sink off. And the whole thing about Rush missing out on their dinner plans had been ridiculous.

So why hadn't I called King out on all of it? Why had I let him leave a man I barely knew alone with me?

I knew the answer before I even finished the question.

Because I trusted him.

Them.

Yeah, *them.*

There was no way my uncle would ever put me in any kind of danger, and I'd heard enough about Rush to know the man was much more than my uncle's employee. So that answered the question about *why* I trusted my uncle, but what about Rush? Why wasn't I hurrying through patching him up and getting him out the door? Why wasn't that tight ball of fear that pretty much lived in my stomach full-time crushing the little butterflies that were dancing around my insides? Why wasn't my first thought... my *only* thought about protecting my secret?

"Do you really believe that?"

Rush's soft voice broke through my confusing thoughts. I turned my head to look at him full-on.

God, he really was beautiful. I could still feel his arms around me as if it had been only yesterday that he'd come to my aid. Night after night, I heard that little hitch in his voice as he reassured me he'd gotten to me on time.

"What?" I asked, not to stall for time but because I really had forgotten what he'd said.

"Do you really not believe in love stories, Christopher?" Rush asked. He leaned forward a bit, but he was careful not to disturb Pip. I was mesmerized by the way his lips moved as he spoke. "That moment when your heart beats just a little bit quicker when you meet someone you know in your gut is different? The nerves that come with those first tentative touches."

Rush paused long enough for me to realize I was staring at his mouth. I forced my eyes up. It turned out his mouth was the safer bet because his eyes burned with something the old me would have fantasized was desire.

"That first kiss?" Rush continued. "The sigh of relief when you know everything is going to be okay. That you're finally going to be getting the happily ever after it feels like you've been waiting your entire life for…?"

I had no clue if he was still talking about the books or something else. This time, I *did* find the need to stall for time to process everything that was happening, so I responded, "Do you?"

Good Lord, why had I asked him that? I'd meant to tell him that no, I didn't believe it… not for me anyway, but as usual, the words I intended to say got mixed up with the ones that formed the question I really wanted an answer to.

Rush smiled softly and glanced down at Pip. His big hand dwarfed the kitten as he continued to pet him. The mere thought of those strong fingers drifting over my skin made my insides feel hot.

When Rush's eyes lifted to meet mine, I felt ensnared.

Trapped.

With no desire to escape.

"Absolutely," Rush said.

His answer shouldn't have lit that little spark inside of me that I'd purposefully doused years earlier. The one I'd worked to snuff out from the moment I'd realized that I'd never be strong enough to search for my own happily ever after.

"Does every love story unfold like they do in those books?" Rush murmured as his eyes shifted toward my kitchen and presumably the three boxes of romance novels sitting on the island. "No, not likely," he continued. "But I think that's the point of those stories... everyone's love story is different." Rush paused for a moment before adding, "Different but no less magical."

I wasn't sure how long I stared at him in mute fascination before I caught myself. "Not everyone gets a happily ever after," I said softly as I pulled out some latex gloves and began putting them on.

"No... no, they don't," Rush agreed.

I could practically feel his eyes on me. It was unnerving, but it didn't scare me. Not like when other men watched me.

I pulled my penlight out of my medical kit and forced myself to look at Rush. He hadn't moved, and I was right about the whole watching thing. I flicked the light on and said, "I want to check the cut to make sure there's no glass in it."

Rush obliged me without a word and leaned forward as much as he could without disturbing Pip. I closed the distance between us and flicked the light up to the wound. I tried to ignore the slight tremble in my hand, but considering there was a bright light bouncing around on Rush's tanned skin, it was pretty much impossible.

"Do you have one?" I blurted before I could stop myself.

What the hell, Christopher?

"One what?" Rush asked, his breath washing over my arm in a whisper of a caress. "A happily ever after? Or a love story?"

"Forget I asked that. It's none of my business," I said quickly as I finished examining the cut and tried to force myself into autopilot mode. A few minutes ago, I'd been hung up on Rush's every word, but now I wanted to escape with what was left of my pride.

I was in the process of reaching for an antiseptic wipe when Rush's fingers ghosted over the arm I hadn't even realized I was resting on his knee. The touch did what Rush had probably intended.

It got my attention.

A hundred and ten percent of it.

"Not yet," he said softly as our eyes met yet again. "Not yet," he repeated even more quietly as his eyes filled with that unnamed emotion that had stopped me short in the club that night.

The reminder of how I'd met the man was the same as being doused with ice water. My skin went cold even as my insides filled with an ugly, terrible heat. My stomach rolled violently as I tried desperately to remain even-keeled. I must have managed it because Rush stopped touching me, and I could feel his eyes shifting away.

Oh God, didn't he know that I needed that little bit of connection? That touch that reminded me I was safe?

"A couple of my exes could put the villains in those books to shame." Rush let out a dry laugh before adding, "One girl actually left a live rabbit in my bed and a pot of water boiling on my stove. Thankfully the rabbit wasn't hurt, but she did trash my apartment.:

I wanted to laugh. I really did. I wanted to ask him what had happened to the rabbit… and the ex.

But to talk I needed to be able to breathe, and it felt like there was a ten-ton weight on my chest.

Please, Christopher, I just want to be with you. I love you.

My stomach cramped hard, and then the telltale sign of saliva began to pool in my mouth. I tried to swallow the sensation back down as I attempted to clumsily climb to my feet.

Unfortunately, Rush chose that moment to close his fingers around my wrist.

"Christopher?"

I shook my head and desperately tried to pull free of his hold, but even if Rush had gotten the clumsy, silent message, it was already too late. As I began retching, I dropped back down on the ottoman and just let it happen.

Let it? Who was I kidding? I had absolutely no control over my body's response to what amounted to nothing more than a few bad memories.

If I *had* had control, I most certainly would have made it to the bathroom before puking my guts out.

Or I would have at least had the sense to expel the contents of my stomach anywhere else besides where the mess ultimately landed.

All over Rush's shoes.

CHAPTER THREE

RUSH

☥4

My heart hurt for Christopher as he continued to vomit until there was nothing left in his system to expel.

As soon as he'd started throwing up, I'd dropped one hand to the back of his neck to support him as best I could. I didn't give a shit that my boots were taking the brunt of it; they'd seen worse.

Christopher's skin felt cold and clammy beneath my palm. It confirmed what I'd already suspected.

The young man wasn't throwing up because he was sick. The episode had been brought on by some event in his mind that I'd likely triggered with all my rambling. Unfortunately, I couldn't figure out what I'd said. But I'd seen the look in his eyes when something had shifted. I'd made the mistake of touching him in the hopes of comforting him, but apparently, I hadn't removed my hand quickly enough.

As the retching stopped, Christopher just hung there for a moment. I let my hand slide down the back of his neck to his shoulder. "Hey," I said softly. "It's okay."

Christopher didn't respond at all other than to wipe his mouth with his still-gloved hand.

"Hey," I repeated in the hopes of getting him to look at me, but instead, Christopher shrugged my hand off his shoulder.

"I'll be right back," he murmured. He stood shakily, but when I tried to stand to assist him, he shook his head. "No, please, can you just... can you wait here?"

There was no denying the need in his voice.

The need to escape.

Knowing he probably wanted to pull himself together both physically and mentally, I let him go. He promptly went to the kitchen and returned with a dish towel, which he handed me. As soon as I took it, he quietly went up the stairs and disappeared for several minutes. I used the time to clean off my boots and the surrounding floor, but since it was an area rug, it was easier said than done. I went to the kitchen to look for any kind of carpet cleaner beneath his sink but couldn't find anything. Since I wasn't about to snoop around his kitchen, I wetted down the towel with water and returned to the living room to clean the mess up as best I could. A quick return to the kitchen had me tossing the dish towel into the sink and then reaching underneath for the dustpan and broom I'd seen earlier.

I made quick work of cleaning up as much of the glass as I could but made a mental note to remind Christopher to vacuum the area just to be sure. I was in the process of dumping the contents of the dustpan into the garbage when I sensed I was no longer alone. Sure enough, Christopher was watching me.

"Hey, you okay?" I asked as I quickly put the dustpan and broom away.

"You didn't need to do that," Christopher murmured as he looked back at the spot where I'd taken out his side table. I'd tossed the broken pieces of wood along the wall as I'd been cleaning up the glass.

"I'll buy you a new one," I said as I motioned to the debris. "Maybe you can send me a link for the store where you got them?"

Christopher shook his head. "It's fine. Can I... Can I finish...?" He motioned to my head.

"Yeah, sure," I responded, though the last thing I was worried about was my head. I followed Christopher back to the living room.

He made sure to steer clear of the soiled part of the carpet and motioned for me to sit. Pip had curled himself up into a tiny ball at the end of the couch, so I took the other end. This time, Christopher sat next to me on the couch, but he was all business. Within two minutes, my wound was cleaned and covered with butterfly bandages.

Christopher climbed to his feet and quickly grabbed all the debris from the supplies before hurrying to the kitchen. I followed but didn't say anything. He was once again the Christopher he'd been when King and I had arrived, and I knew in my gut that nothing I said would get through to the old Christopher.

"I'll pay to have your boots professionally cleaned, or if you prefer, I can buy you new ones," the young man said as he began wiping down the already spotless countertop. It was likely just an excuse to keep his back to me.

"No worries, they've seen worse," I said softly. "Christopher?"

"Make sure to put an ice pack on the back of your shoulder. And leave the butterflies on for a few days. Take some ibuprofen when you get home. That will help with your head and your shoulder. If you feel any kind of nausea or anything, go to the ER just to be on the safe side. There was no LOC, but cerebral edema is always possible with head injuries."

"Christopher…"

Although Christopher hadn't stopped moving throughout his speech, as soon as I said his name again, he did. But he wouldn't look at me. It made me feel empty.

Lost.

"Thanks for patching me up. Next time, I'll try not to do a half gainer on any of your furniture or your cat."

I'd hoped the comment would make him turn around, but there was no change in his frame. His back was ramrod straight, and his shoulders were locked tight. He didn't even look at me.

"You take care, Christopher," I murmured before turning my back on him and heading to the front door. I heard the kitchen faucet turn on, so I knew there wasn't a possibility that he was following me to see me out.

I made quick work of leaving the small house and then headed east. As I'd suspected, King was waiting for me at the end of the block. I'd been pretty sure my friend hadn't completely ditched me like he'd pretended. As I took in the sight of King leaning with his back against the front of the vehicle, I couldn't really be angry with him.

King barely reacted as I walked around the front of the truck and leaned against it. I almost smiled when I saw him toying with his handgun. He was ejecting the clip and reloading it over and over. It was a nervous habit he'd engaged in from the time I'd met him, but I hadn't seen him doing it for a while now.

Not since he and Gio had gotten together.

"You need a new nervous habit, buddy. That one's going to land you in jail," I said.

King sighed and put the gun away. "Did he tell you anything?" the man asked as he glanced at me.

"Was he supposed to?"

King pushed away from the car and began pacing in front of it. "When I saw him jump into action after you fell... I don't know, I just thought..." King fell silent and shook his head.

I straightened and then went to grab my friend's arm to stop his forward movement. I opened my hand. "Keys," I said. "You owe me a drink."

King didn't argue with me. He handed the keys over, and within ten minutes, we were sitting in a dive bar in a part of Seattle I wasn't familiar with but that certainly didn't cater to the tourist business. I ordered us a couple of beers and joined King in one of the few booths available in the place.

When King didn't say anything, I said, "So you left me in there to do some kind of recon on your nephew?"

"Yeah, I suppose I did." King took a long pull on his beer and then added, "He's not Christopher anymore. Hasn't been in a long time."

"You said he went to nursing school, right?"

King nodded. "One of the best. Duke. It had an accelerated BSN program. He stayed here for his undergrad, then went to Duke and got his BSN in just sixteen months. The plan was for him to do the nurse practitioner program through Duke via distance learning, which meant he'd only have to spend a week in North Carolina every semester, and the rest he'd do from home."

"What changed?" I asked.

King shrugged. "None of us can fucking figure it out. He's just not... our Christopher." King took another drink. "He had all these plans, Rush. He knew what he wanted from the time he was a kid, and he was doing it. Nursing, Duke, all of it. But something had been different about him for a while. He stopped interacting with the family as much, especially after he left Seattle. But when he got back a few months ago, he was... a stranger."

I couldn't help but agree that the title was a fitting one.

"How so?" I asked.

"He wouldn't come to family functions, wouldn't even talk to Micah or Con. They called, they stopped by his house which he'd bought on his own without even telling anyone. And he never enrolled in the nurse practitioner program. He works remotely for an insurance company processing claims. He has all his groceries delivered, he never invites anyone to stay if they come for a visit. Hell, he's remodeling the place and hasn't asked for help. And those books..."

"The romances?" I clarified.

King nodded. "He loved those books. He's probably got thousands more on his Kindle. The ones we took over are the ones he read when he was real young... He'd get them from thrift shops for pennies on the dollar using coins he found lying around the house or on the street. Even though he could have gotten them on his Kindle once he was older, he still hung on to those paperbacks."

"They meant something to him," I observed.

"Yeah," King murmured. "Con and Micah had been storing them while Christopher was gone, but when they brought them over here along with Christopher's other stuff, he told them to throw them away. Gio and I took them instead because we both knew how much he loved those books."

"Tough love," I murmured as I remembered that had been King's plan when we'd taken the books over. "That turned out to not be so tough."

King didn't respond, and I hadn't expected him to. My friend was a cold-blooded, chillingly dangerous man when it came to dealing with murderers, rapists, and sex traffickers, but around his family, he was totally different. He was the man who'd pleaded with Christopher to talk to him tonight.

"I shouldn't have blindsided you like that, Rush," King said with a sigh. "But when I saw a little bit of the old Christopher, I just thought…"

"I saw it too, King," I said. "The old and the new. Your Christopher is still in there." I was reluctant to say any more since I felt like what had transpired between myself and his nephew was private and needed to stay between us.

"This is going to kill Gio," King whispered.

"Christopher and Gio don't talk?" I asked. "They've been best friends for years, haven't they?"

"They talk… but it's not real. It's Gio talking through the walls Christopher had put up, so the only things that get through are the simple, polite crap. 'How are you? Can you believe all this rain? Fettucine is good.'"

Fettucine was Gio and King's mastiff. If the conversations between the two friends had come down to discussing the dog's antics, then yeah, something was really fucked-up between them.

"Did all of this start after that night in the club?" I asked.

King nodded. "But it was still the old Christopher then. He was just… just quieter if that makes sense."

I dipped my head because it made perfect sense. The reality was that they wouldn't have been in that club if Gio hadn't gone looking for King. I had no doubt Gio blamed himself as did King. It also wouldn't have surprised me in the least to know that Christopher carried just as much guilt.

"We tried to get Christopher to talk to a professional about it, especially after what happened to him when he was a kid, but he kept saying he was fine."

I shook my head. There was no way the young man could be fine after not one, but two violent assaults that had barely been stopped in time. Just because he'd escaped being penetrated hadn't meant he didn't carry the scars of those attacks day in and day out.

"He was legally an adult," I responded. "There was nothing else you could have done."

King's eyes shifted briefly to mine.

I nodded and said, "Yeah, I know, it's a bullshit line that doesn't make anyone feel better."

We sat there in silence for a moment before King said, "Come on, we should get going. Gio's going to want to know what happened."

I could already see the pained expression in King's eyes as he had to contemplate telling his fiancé that Christopher was still as lost to them as ever. I followed King out of the bar and rode out the silence in the cab of his truck as he drove me to my hotel. I was so lost in thought that I didn't even notice we'd arrived until King said, "Thanks again, Rush. I'll call you tomorrow."

"Yeah," I said as I climbed out of the car and watched King drive off.

It's not your problem.

It's not your problem.

Even as the warning played on a loop inside of my head as I made my way to my hotel room, I laughed because nothing could be further from the truth.

Whatever was happening with Christopher was most definitely my problem.

I just didn't know why.

CHAPTER FOUR

CHRISTOPHER

♂4

I saw him coming long before he knocked on the door thanks to the cameras I'd installed strategically outside the house.

So I *could* have ignored him. I *could* have put my headphones back on my head and continued on with the claim I'd been working on. I *could* have done anything at all besides answer the door when there was a sharp knock on it. Even knowing what Rush was carrying didn't make a difference. So then why were my fingers closing around the doorknob? Why was that little spark of energy in my stomach turning into the dreaded butterflies?

My curiosity outweighed my common sense, and before I knew it, there was nothing standing between me and Rush except for what looked like a table similar to the one Rush had broken.

"I've already tested this one, and I'm glad to say it's Rush-proof," Rush said before I could even open my mouth.

"It's beautiful," I admitted as my eyes took in the rich, deep tone of the wood. It was definitely real wood and not the fake stuff my table had been made up of. And the design of the table screamed antique.

Antiques meant money.

"You didn't have to," I said with a sigh. "Thank you, Rush, but I can't accept it. It must have cost you—"

"It didn't," Rush cut in. "I, um…"

The uncertainty in his voice had me lifting my eyes. A wave of vulnerability and hurt washed over his expression before he dropped his eyes to the table so I couldn't see them anymore.

"It belonged to my parents," he said softly. "I think they would have liked for you to have it."

His comment didn't make much sense, but the hurt in his voice did.

"Come in," I said quickly as I pulled the door open farther. I made sure to pick up Pip so he wouldn't cause another accident. I watched in silence as Rush carried the weighty side table inside and placed it in the spot the other one had been in. I caught my breath at how perfect the piece of furniture looked.

"Rush," I said with a shake of my head. "At least let me pay you—"

"Christopher, I've got three storage units full of my parents' belongings. Everyone kept telling me to sell it all off in an estate sale before I left Colorado, but I couldn't do that."

The raw pain in Rush's voice as he spoke had me moving closer to him. I wanted to offer some kind of comfort for the loss he was so clearly still dealing with, but I didn't know how.

"You weren't ready to let them go," I suggested.

Rush nodded. "I've got the stuff from my own apartment in another unit, so when I get my own place, I'll do some mixing and matching and sell or donate what's left. I like knowing that a piece of my parents is here with you, even if it's just so you can tell someone the story about the clumsy idiot who broke your original table."

I found myself smiling. And then I did something I hadn't been planning. I cuddled Pip with one arm and stepped into Rush and wrapped the other around him. I couldn't say who was more surprised at the move, him or me, but before I could try and undo it, Rush's head was dropping to my shoulder and his arm was going around my waist.

Alarm bells should have been going crazy in my head, but there was nothing but silence. There was no obsessive, insistent voice reminding me that the man could be reading too much into the gesture, and there wasn't the perpetual sense of loss I felt when one of my family members managed to get their arms around me for a hug.

It wasn't until Rush lifted his head and a few pregnant, silent beats followed that it became like someone had flipped a switch and all the easiness was sucked out of the room, only to be replaced by this heavy tension that had nothing to do with discomfort or awkwardness.

I willed myself not to look at his mouth, but that was exactly what I did. My body went haywire the second I took in Rush's full lips, and it wasn't until Pip let out a little squeak that I realized how much my body had locked up tight in anticipation of what was to come. To cover my behavior, I shoved Pip at Rush, giving him no choice but to take the kitten, and hurried to the kitchen. "I'm just going to get something to dust it off a bit."

I sensed Rush's eyes on me as I moved around the kitchen in search of a suddenly missing dish towel, but I couldn't find it.

"I used it to clean up yesterday," I heard Rush say from behind me. As he spoke, he moved around the island so I could see him since the boxes of books were still in the same place. "I'm not sure if that's the one you're looking for…"

"It is," I acknowledged. "I threw it in the laundry basket."

I pressed my back against the sink as he approached me. I couldn't say if I was happy or disappointed when all he did was hand me Pip.

Rush took several steps back and leaned his back against the edge of the island, leaving only a few feet between us.

"I could offer to take my shirt off and use that to wipe it down, but that sounds like the beginning of a bad porno movie."

The comment was so out of the blue that I let out a shocked little laugh. It was only when I saw the mischief dancing in his eyes that I realized he'd said the words for that exact effect.

"Do they even call them pornos anymore?" I asked. "How old are you exactly?"

"Touché," Rush said with a smile.

I couldn't resist the smile that crossed my own mouth. The only one I'd ever bantered with in any kind of way had been Gio, and that had been a long time ago. The mere thought of what I'd let my relationship with Gio become made something inside of me hurt. I eased Pip to the floor and then turned to face the sink and turned the water on. My hands didn't need washing, but I needed a moment to get control of my wayward emotions. When I turned around though, Rush hadn't politely moved away, and he hadn't stopped looking at me with those all-knowing eyes of his.

"Where did you go just now?" he asked.

"Nowhere," I easily lied.

God, I'd become way too good at that. Not necessarily telling lies people believed but being able to just spout one off without giving my conscience even another thought.

I could tell Rush didn't believe me, but I was glad when he didn't press the issue. He glanced toward the wall that separated the kitchen area from the dining area. "Are you remodeling?" he asked.

"Um, yeah… no… I don't know," I said with a laugh. "They make taking a wall down look a lot easier on TV."

Rush smiled. "They do. My father would go crazy when he watched those shows. Kind of like when a cop watches a police show or something."

"Your dad worked in construction?" I asked.

That sadness he'd been wearing when he'd talked about the table fell over him again, but there was also a lightness in his eyes as he confronted his memories.

"He was a contractor. Built his business from the ground up. He was hands-on, and he never left a customer unhappy. Didn't matter how big or small the job was. 'Treat every job like it's the one that's putting food on your table, son, because sometimes it is.'"

"Smart man," I said softly.

"He was."

"And your mom?" I dared to ask.

"Had him wrapped around her finger," Rush responded. We both laughed at that, but then Rush went quiet again. "She worked in a nursing home. Even after Dad's business blew up and there was enough money to do anything or nothing, she never missed a day of work. Every single one of her patients was family, and my mom never turned her back on family."

The last few words of his statement caused a sharp pain to slice through my gut. Rush must have noticed because he said, "Fuck, Christopher—"

"It's okay," I said even as my heart dropped out. The mere fact that he knew why I was upset was telling. "He told you, didn't he?"

Rush fell silent for a moment. "He told me you and your family aren't as close as you used to be and that they're all worried about you."

What did you think was going to happen, Christopher? Rainbows and unicorns and some cheesy happily ever after?

I welcomed the ugly voice's return. Cynical, bitter Christopher never failed to make his presence known if the old me tried to resurface for too long.

"Well, at least I'm getting something out of the deal," I murmured as I glanced toward the new table. "Do I have to provide some kind of proof that I'm still the naïve, sweet kid I used to be, or will they take your word for it?"

"It's not—"

I wasn't interested in hearing anything else that he had to say, so I made a move to leave the kitchen, but Rush's fingers closed around my left wrist. I hated the warmth that flowed through all the spots where his skin met mine.

"Let go," I demanded, though I didn't try to pull free of him. He was way too big and strong to risk pissing off.

"Your family has no idea I'm here."

"I don't care," I said as the fear inside of me began to grow. If I couldn't drive him away with my words…

"Christopher…"

"I asked you to go," I repeated sternly as I leaned my weight away from him in the hopes that he'd get the hint and release me. He ended up doing just that, but I hadn't really believed he'd give up so easily, so when he did let go, I lost my balance and fell backward. I threw my right hand out to catch myself on the counter at the same time that

Rush made a grab for me. My right hand scrabbled for purchase when it hit the metal drying rack on the counter. Without thinking, I closed my hand around the highest part of the rack—the utensil holder—thinking it would somehow help me get my balance. Unfortunately, instead of the holder itself, my hand closed around the blade of the large knife I'd rinsed off and put into the holder *blade up* just minutes before Rush's arrival.

The knife slicing through my palm took a few seconds to register. There wasn't even any real pain. It was the blood that my brain was trying to adjust to. It flowed down my wrist and dripped onto the floor, leaving me in a dreamlike state.

It doesn't look any different, I heard the old, logical Christopher say. I didn't hear much from him anymore. I was kind of glad about that.

It wasn't until I heard Rush say, "Oh shit, Christopher!" and felt his fingers closing around the wrist of my uninjured hand that I came back to the present. "Here, let's get some water on it," Rush ordered as he tugged me toward the sink. He had the water going before I knew it, and then he was reaching for my injured hand.

His clean, bare skin and my tainted blood.

"Let me see," Rush said gently as he began to close his fingers over my hand.

"Don't!" I screamed at the top of my lungs. I yanked my hand away from him and stepped back and promptly slipped on something wet. Probably my own blood.

"Christopher, it's okay," Rush said calmly like he was talking to an enraged toddler. He reached for me again even though I'd managed to catch myself on the counter.

"No, don't," I repeated. But his hand kept up its forward movement, and the warning was out of my mouth before I could even consider the consequences.

"Rush, don't touch my blood! My viral count isn't undetectable yet!"

CHAPTER FIVE

RUSH

44

Despite all the personal issues I'd had with the military, in that moment I had to admit to being grateful for every ounce of training they'd drilled into me because that discipline and focus were the only things that made it possible to both process Christopher's words and to react to them appropriately.

"You could have microscopic cuts on your fingers," Christopher said in a rush. "You can't touch me."

I put my hands up to show Christopher I wasn't going to. His relief was palpable.

"Put your hand under the water," I ordered before striding out of the kitchen. It didn't take me long to find what I was looking for because it was still sitting in the same place in the living room that it had been the day before.

Christopher's medical kit.

I snatched the thing off the floor and hurried back to the kitchen.

During those thirty seconds, the reality of what the young man had told me hit me like a ton of bricks.

He's HIV positive.

A soul-crushing sadness began to wash over me, but I forced it away. The last thing Christopher needed was pity. If and when he needed a shoulder to lean on, I'd be first in line, but for now, I needed to focus on the immediate problem.

"How does it look?" I asked as I returned to the kitchen. Christopher jumped.

"You're still here," he said in genuine surprise.

"Um, yeah, where did you think—"

I stopped abruptly when I realized what it was he'd been thinking. That I'd left him because of what he'd told me.

I practically slammed the medical kit down on the counter next to the sink. "We're going to talk about that later," I said stiffly as I searched out the latex gloves I was hoping to find.

As I worked them on, Christopher said, "Rush, you don't have to. The cut's not that bad, so I can handle it by myself."

I ignored his words as I rummaged around the kitchen for a clean towel. As soon as I found one, I returned to his side and muttered, "I guess you've been doing a lot of that these days, haven't you?"

As much as I'd tried to keep the anger out of my voice, I hadn't been totally successful. I had no doubt at all that he hadn't told anyone in his family what was going on. He, who had one of the most supportive and loving families I'd ever met, hadn't leaned on them when he'd needed to the most.

His physical state made more sense now as well. The stress alone would have explained the weight loss and haggard appearance, but it could also just as easily be the illness or any medications he was taking to combat it.

He'd said his viral count wasn't undetectable yet, which meant he was likely taking medication, but if it wasn't working, then he could very well be past the point...

My stomach dropped out violently, but I just as quickly shook my head.

No. Not happening. Not him.

I forced myself to focus on the problem at hand. I turned the water off and then gently pulled Christopher's hand toward me and pressed the dish towel against it to add pressure. It didn't take long for blood to seep through the fabric. That in itself was telling, but I pulled the towel back for a moment to confirm what I already suspected.

"It's going to need stitches," I said on a sigh.

Christopher merely nodded like he already knew.

I went and grabbed another dish towel and swapped it out with the bloodstained one. "Put pressure on this," I instructed. I found a roll of bandaging in the kit, so I used that to secure the towel to Christopher's hand. Christopher was silent throughout all of it, but I didn't miss his wince when I had to add pressure to the wound by tightening the bandaging. "Sorry," I heard myself whisper each time he did it. By the time it was done, I wasn't sure who was more relieved, him or me.

"Come on, I'll drive you to the hospital," I said as I removed the gloves and tossed them in the garbage.

"It's okay, I can get an Uber or something," Christopher responded. He turned his back on me and went to the drying rack to remove the large knife he'd cut his hand on. "No wonder my uncle always put the blades down in the dishwasher," he said flatly. He put the knife in the sink and then reached into the cabinets below.

"Hey," I said to stop him. I grabbed his elbow at the same time. "What do you need?" I asked.

"Bleach," he responded tiredly.

I grabbed the bottle he was pointing at, but instead of giving it to him, I uncapped it and poured a hefty amount of the liquid over the knife. I reached for the rest of the utensils in the drying tray and dumped the container of them into the sink, then doused them all in bleach. "We can wash them better once we get back," I said.

"Rush—"

"My truck's parked in the driveway," I continued in my "I'm not taking shit from anyone" voice. I closed the distance between us and motioned toward the doorway.

Christopher let out a resigned sigh and then began moving. As I followed him out of the house, I couldn't stop touching him. His lower back, his shoulders, his elbow. The moves probably looked like I was just trying to assist him, but the truth was that I *needed* to touch him.

I opened the passenger door for a now silent Christopher. It was like he'd tuned me out at some point because he didn't even react when I had to reach across his body to belt him in. It wasn't until I was in the driver's seat and putting my car into gear that he finally spoke.

"Can I borrow your phone? I left mine upstairs next to my computer."

I pulled the phone from my pocket, unlocked it, and handed it to him. He looked something up on the browser, then clicked on a phone number.

"Hey, Anita, it's Christopher. I, um, cut my hand and was hoping Dr. Kleinman could—" Christopher went silent for a moment as he listened to the speaker on the other end, and then he was nodding. "Thanks, we'll be there in about twenty minutes. See you then. Bye."

Christopher hung up, and then he was pulling the address up on my phone and turning on the GPS so the phone could guide me to the destination. The fact that he didn't want to tell me himself wasn't a good sign.

But I couldn't let him off that easy. Sure, I had a million questions, but those could wait. I needed him to keep talking to me, even if it had nothing to do with the events of today. If he stopped talking, then I would become another person he'd hide from.

And I didn't think Christopher could afford to hide himself away from even one other person.

"Is Dr. Kleinman your primary care doctor?" I asked.

There was a long, awkward silence, but instead of letting the question go like Christopher clearly wanted me to, I kept glancing his way.

"No, um, she's a specialist."

As in, a specialist who treated infectious diseases like HIV.

"And she'll be able to see you as soon as we get there?" I probed.

Christopher nodded. I was surprised when he continued on his own with "Even if there isn't a long wait at the ER, sometimes the staff who work there, they look at you like…"

"Like what?" I asked gently.

Christopher let out a soft sigh. He began rubbing his uninjured palm over his knee. "Like you're dirty," he whispered.

"Christopher—" I began, but he continued as if I hadn't spoken.

"It's not all of them. Most are really professional, but you can always get someone who…" Christopher shook his head. "I've only had it happen to me once, but in school when we'd shadow the ER, I saw it happen a few times. And some of the people in my graduating class made it clear they hoped to never run into one of us during their careers."

One of *us*.

That one little word spoke volumes. I could feel the anger vibrating through me as I thought about anyone hurting Christopher like that. He was literally one of the sweetest, most caring people I'd ever met and I barely even knew him.

"Rush, why did you leave the army?"

"How did you know I left?" I asked, completely caught off guard by the change of subject.

Christopher was staring at his bandaged hand. When he didn't answer, I realized what the question was really about. He was feeling vulnerable and exposed. I'd just learned what likely amounted to the biggest secret he'd ever had, and he was undoubtedly terrified of what I would do with the information. No doubt he knew how many questions I had, and before I could ask them, he wanted to know if I was willing to expose my own jugular a bit.

"I was a coward," I admitted.

Christopher's head jerked in my direction. "I don't believe that," he said firmly.

I was silent for a moment as I acknowledged the warmth that had come from his instant defense of me. "A hundred people could tell me otherwise, but it only matters what I tell myself, you know?" I explained.

"Yeah," Christopher responded solemnly. "I know."

That comment would definitely need some following up.

"So you were afraid you were going to die," Christopher murmured.

"Yes, but I think that's pretty much a given for most people."

"Then why did you call yourself a… *that*."

The fact that he couldn't refer to me as a coward in any way would have made me smile if the conversation wasn't so serious to begin with.

"From the second you step off that bus for boot camp, you have to give yourself over entirely. The army becomes your mother and father, your unit your brothers. Orders don't get questioned. *Ever.* Doesn't matter if you know it's some clueless bureaucrat handing them down or if command doesn't have all of the intel or even the right intel… you get the order to pull that trigger or call in a drone strike or whatever, you do it. No questions asked. You have to assume whoever is giving you that command knows something you don't. If they tell you a woman is carrying a bomb under her robes, you aren't allowed to see the baby she's carrying in her arms. You put a bullet through that kid's brain to get to hers if that's your only shot. You don't worry about that kid hitting the ground headfirst when its mother drops from your kill shot. You pull the trigger."

"Did that happen to you?" Christopher asked.

"No," I said with a shake of the head. "But I saw it happen to a buddy. Only he *didn't* pull the trigger like he was ordered to, and the woman detonated a bomb that killed over thirty people, including seven men from our unit and her own little girl. My buddy took his own life as soon as he returned stateside."

"I'm sorry," Christopher said softly. I could feel his eyes on me.

"I couldn't do it," I admitted. I was surprised by the emotion that came over me. "I couldn't end one life without knowing in my gut that doing so would save another."

"So you didn't re-enlist," Christopher offered. "You started working with Uncle King instead. Saving kids."

I shot Christopher a glance. He'd turned in his seat a bit so he could look at me rather than through the windshield. His tousled dark blond hair made his skin look even paler, but there was no doubting he was completely engaged in the conversation. He really did want to know this stuff about me. I tried to ignore the sparks of excitement in my belly as I wondered what that meant.

"Rush?"

Christopher's quiet, worried voice broke through my own confusing thoughts.

"Sorry," I responded. "So you know about all that?"

"About the kids and what my family does for them?"

"Yeah."

Christopher nodded. "It may have all started with Gio, but it didn't end when he came home. There are too many other kids out there waiting for someone to come for them. There are too many terrified, desperate parents who are clinging to every last ounce of hope they have that they will see their child again."

His poignant words had me silently nodding because that was exactly why we did what we did. Years earlier, King and his brothers of the heart had been like any other family in the world; they'd been living their lives, completely unprepared for what fate had planned for them. One of the brothers, Luca, who shared no blood with King but called him best friend, had lost his son, Gio, to sex traffickers when the boy was only around eight. What had followed had been a hellish search by all the brothers. Thankfully, with the help of a group of like-minded men and women, they'd been able to bring Gio home, but he'd been only one of thousands of kids waiting for their own rescue to come.

"Well said," I murmured in response to Christopher's words. "So you wanted to know about what happened after I left the military. After my tour ended, I was a little lost. I knew I could go home to Colorado and join my dad's business, but I knew it wasn't something I really wanted. My dad did too."

As I thought about my father, a stab of pain swept through me.

The man had been my biggest champion, and my mother had been right there next to him cheering at the top of her lungs.

"Rush?" Christopher said softly, and then I felt his fingers touching mine. Not entirely believing it was really happening, I looked down to confirm it, and sure enough, his uninjured hand was resting against my own.

I must have been staring too long at our nearly joined hands because Christopher began to pull his hand away, his expression uncertain. At the same time, someone honked their horn at me because the traffic light had turned green. I closed my fingers around Christopher's as I got the car moving. When he didn't try and pull away, I linked our fingers.

"I thought they'd be ashamed of me," I admitted.

"Who? Your parents? For leaving the army?"

I nodded.

"They weren't," Christopher said without hesitation. It wasn't a question, and he didn't seem to be looking for confirmation. As far as he was concerned, he was just stating a fact.

"How do you know?" I asked in surprise. The young man was an enigma, and I was enjoying peeling back all the layers that made him so much more than what he appeared to be at first glance.

"They raised you into the man you are, Rush. There's nothing cowardly about doing what was right for you. Being who you are. You loved them very much. That's obvious from the way you talk about them... from the heart. You had to learn that from somewhere. They were proud of you. I don't need to have met them to know that."

I found myself squeezing his fingers just a bit harder. "You're right. They were very proud of me for following my heart."

Christopher nodded his head like he'd won a bet. I found myself smiling. "How's your hand feeling?"

"Starting to feel it now," he admitted.

"We'll be there in a few minutes," I said. I paused and then added, "Soooooo, you never answered my question," I pointed out.

Christopher looked at me in confusion.

"How did you know I left the army after my first tour?"

When his cheeks reddened, I felt my insides jump, though I had no idea why. Maybe the idea of him thinking about me even once after we'd first met appealed to me.

More than it should.

"Christopher?" I said in mock warning. "Spill."

CHAPTER SIX

CHRISTOPHER

☦4

I couldn't make sense of how I'd gotten myself into this mess.

Any of it.

First off, to be so stupid as to even let Rush get close enough to me for physical contact to be an issue…that had been off-the-charts stupid.

But then to flounder about like a dying fish and land on the sharpest object in the vicinity simply because the man released me exactly like I'd asked…

And now this.

Damn it. When would my words and my brain agree on things *before* I said them out loud? Especially around this man?

Okay, well, truth be told, that particular problem seemed to *only* occur around this man.

And if all that hadn't been bad enough, to then go and admit the secret I'd been hiding for the last six months of my life…

I knew he was going to ask me about the HIV. I knew I was going to have to beg him not to, just like I was going to have to beg him with everything I was not to tell my family.

My heart began to pound in my chest. Each painful thud was accompanied by a sharp, stabbing pain in my head. I closed my eyes in an attempt to stave off the tornado of emotions that wanted to spill from my throat.

The same ones I'd kept imprisoned from the moment the doctor had sealed my fate with a few simple words that alone meant nothing but together meant everything.

"Christopher?"

Rush's voice was full of concern, and his hold on my hand almost bordered on painful. But I welcomed his firm grip. I used it to try and ground myself.

It just wasn't enough.

"Did it live?" I managed to grate out, even though it felt like broken glass was being raked along my brain.

"What—?" Rush asked worriedly. I managed to look at Rush as the car slowed down and he began letting out soft curses as one car horn after another went off behind us. I figured it had something to do with me. I suspected he was trying to find a place to pull over.

"Rush," I managed to call out. "I'm okay," I lied.

"The fuck you are," Rush growled. "You look like you're going to fucking pass out—"

It was only when Rush began to pull his fingers free of mine that I truly began to panic. I saw him grab his cellphone.

"Rush, please" was all I managed to get out as flames of unbearable heat pulsed throughout my entire body.

I must have finally gotten something right in just those two little words because Rush dropped his phone in the cup holder and then covered my hand with his. The car began to speed up again, and the horns stopped.

"Did it live?" I repeated. "The rabbit?" Just speaking those few words felt like it had taken every ounce of energy in my body.

"The rabbit," Rush softly repeated. The concern in his voice was apparent, but he had a calmness about him that helped slow my racing heart and eased the pounding in my head. "Yeah, she did. I named her Thumper because it was the only rabbit name I could think of besides Bugs, who was clearly a guy, and the Energizer Bunny, which was just wrong..."

Despite the direction his answer was taking, I couldn't help but find it both amusing and relaxing.

"I was fully expecting to find a horse's head in my bed after that… well, not a real head or anything, but Catrice was a huge fan of movies, so nothing was really off the table when it came to her getting back at me. Creative *and* vengeful… not the best of combinations."

As the pain in my body began to fall away, leaving only the stinging in my hand, my lids began to feel heavy. In truth, all of me felt heavy… like cement blocks were tied around each limb. But something about Rush's voice made all of that fade to the background.

"Did you keep her?" I managed to ask.

"Catrice? Hell no, kicked her ass to the curb real quick. Crazy bitch said she'd call the cops if I didn't give her back the rabbit." Rush let out a little laugh.

"What did you do?" I asked.

"I let her."

I chuckled. "What happened?"

"I got rid of her for good when she found out she was facing jail time, I got to keep Thumper, and one of the cops gave me his number. He and I dated for six months before we mutually agreed it was over. Guess what he gave me as a parting gift."

I closed my eyes and smiled. "What?"

"Guess," Rush prodded.

My brain felt too foggy to do anything more than tell my body to keep converting oxygen into carbon dioxide, but I managed to throw out a nonsense answer. "A rabbit."

When Rush didn't respond, I opened my eyes and lifted them. He was shifting his eyes between me and the road. The little grin on his mouth reminded me of the Cheshire cat.

"Oh my God, am I right?" I asked in disbelief.

Rush nodded. He looked so light and happy that it made all the things that usually felt cold inside of me a little less so.

"After that, it became this running joke. Whenever one of my relationships ended, if the guy or girl didn't give me a rabbit, my parents made sure to."

I laughed. "How many did you end up with?"

"Five," Rush responded. He had to wait until I was done laughing before he added, "Thankfully, after that, they switched over to stuffed animals because of the whole 'fuck like bunnies' thing. Turns out that shit's true. I probably found homes for more than forty bunny babies before I managed to get the single boy bunny fixed."

I shook my head before resting it on the seat. I was still sitting in a way that I was facing Rush rather than the dashboard, but I didn't care. I liked looking at him. I couldn't believe I'd even once thought of him as a cool, aloof guy who masked his emotions. Maybe he was like that while he worked, but aside from the first minute or two when I'd met him four years ago, I felt like I'd been privy to parts of the man not everyone was fortunate enough to experience.

It doesn't hurt that he's into men as well as women.

I waited for Ugly Christopher to shoot down Old Christopher's spark of hope, but it didn't happen.

It didn't matter, though, because Logical Christopher was present and ready to remind me that even if by some miracle, the older, gorgeous ex-soldier were interested in me, nothing could happen.

I forced my wayward thoughts back to the present. Rush continued to cast me glances as he drove. I tried to think of something, anything to say, but it was like every cell in my body was lost in the way Rush moved, in the way his eyes shone, in the sensation of his fingers rubbing over mine.

I didn't think it could have gotten any better, but it did because Rush released my hand and then reached up to run a knuckle down my cheek. We must have been at a traffic light or something because Rush's gaze lingered on me as he caressed my skin. Shivers of delight crackled beneath my skin as my heart thudded painfully in my chest for a whole other reason.

"Get some rest, Christopher. We still have a few minutes before we get there."

It was like my body was wired to respond to his commands. With just a few strokes of his knuckle and that soft command, my eyes were once again shut, and I could feel the fingers of sleep reaching for me. But there was still a question lingering in my brain.

A question I probably wouldn't have asked if I'd been a hundred percent in my right mind.

"Rush?" I said softly.

"Yeah?" he responded just as quietly. The car was moving again, but he continued to stroke my cheek.

"Did you ever find it? What you were looking for with the men and women?"

"You mean love?" Rush asked.

I nodded because I couldn't repeat the word myself. Maybe because I was afraid of the answer or maybe because it was a concept I'd given up on long ago, I didn't know.

"Not yet."

I shouldn't have been relieved. I shouldn't have been anything. But I couldn't deny the little ball of happy that settled in my belly.

The same ball of happy that popped not three seconds later when Rush spoke his next words just as the darkness of sleep lured me under its spell.

"But I think all of that is about to change."

CHAPTER SEVEN

RUSH

ᛏ4

I f I'd been asleep, the alarm on my phone would have done its job and woken me up, but it wasn't necessary because I'd been up all night watching Christopher sleep.

He was a peaceful sleeper. He was *at peace* when he slept.

So different than when he was awake.

I couldn't even imagine what the young man had been through in the last days, weeks, and months. I still knew nothing about how bad his condition was and part of me didn't want to know. That part of me was terrified.

I hadn't been sure if Christopher had heard me in the car right before he'd fallen asleep when I'd basically told him I was starting to have feelings for him.

I didn't even know how it had happened, I just knew it was different from what I'd felt before as I'd slogged through the heaven and hell of the dating pool.

The excitement I usually felt when I first met someone I was attracted to had been fun and easy. But with Christopher, it was like my entire body was consumed with the sensation. It and every other emotion or reaction to the young man were amplified by a thousand.

It scared me.

A lot.

Like I'd told Christopher, I hadn't been in love before, but I'd hoped for it. I supposed a lot of that had to do with how much in love with each other my parents had been. From the day they'd first met to the last day they'd spent together on this earth, they'd loved each other. Sure, they'd fought like any other couple, and I could remember a few occasions where my father had ended up on the couch for the night, but there had never been any doubt that they were soul mates.

Each other's missing half.

It was a lot for any man or woman to live up to, but I also knew better than to settle. I'd had plenty of opportunities to do just that, but I'd been smart enough to know that trying to spend a lifetime with someone who wasn't that other part of me would only end in disaster and a lot of hurt and anger.

Now, as I watched Christopher sleep, I couldn't help but be glad I'd never settled.

I silenced the alarm on my phone and then reached for the glass of water I'd already grabbed from the kitchen. As I approached the bed, my eyes skimmed over the handful of prescription pill bottles on the nightstand. I already knew which ones he needed to take when. I'd practically studied each bottle after getting Christopher settled the night before.

We hadn't really talked after Christopher had returned to the waiting room. His hand had been freshly bandaged, and he'd had a goofy grin on his face from whatever pain reliever he'd been given. Thankfully, the nurse who'd escorted Christopher had provided me with written instructions on what to watch out for as well as a prescription for additional pain medication. But it had been as I'd been escorting Christopher to the door that Dr. Kleinman had appeared to remind Christopher to stick to his medication schedule. As soon as Christopher had clumsily nodded his head, the doctor had turned to me and practically ordered me to stay with Christopher until he was fully alert and to make sure to give him his medications at the exact times.

Even if I hadn't literally been following doctor's orders, I wouldn't have left Christopher alone. Not when he was so vulnerable. Upon returning to his house after getting the prescription filled, I'd coaxed Christopher into eating some soup I'd found in his kitchen cabinets, and then I'd helped him get ready for bed. He'd been pretty out of it, so he hadn't fought me on anything, and he hadn't asked me to leave. Once he'd taken his meds, he'd been out within a matter of minutes, and I'd settled into a not-so-comfortable chair in the corner of the room that seemed to mostly be for his clothes. Pip had kept me company for a while before abandoning me to sleep in the comfort of his owner's warmth.

I could easily say I'd never been so envious of a cat before.

I sighed and sat on the edge of the bed near Christopher's hip. Pip immediately came to me, but instead of trying to crawl onto me, he peered over the edge of the bed. I got the silent message and lifted him and gently placed him on the ground. The kitten headed for the closet, where I figured his litter box probably was.

Turning my attention back to Christopher, I put the glass on the nightstand and then gave in to my need to touch him. I stroked my finger over his cheekbone, which was just a bit too prominent. I'd definitely need to make sure he started getting more calories in his system.

I allowed my finger to roam over every part of his face. His silky eyebrows, his perfectly shaped nose, his soft eyelids with lush lashes that matched the color of his hair. It wasn't until I reached Christopher's lips that I hesitated. I'd already taken liberties that I shouldn't have. Not to mention the fact that I was already obsessed with his lips. If I knew what they felt like beneath my finger, I'd never be able to keep from tasting him.

I started to pull my finger back with the intent of calling out Christopher's name to wake him up when Christopher's uninjured hand came up to cover mine, keeping my finger in contact with his skin. I flicked my eyes up to see that his own were open and full of something that had my insides tightening and my dick twitching excitedly.

Need.

Not just desire… *need.*

Since Christopher's eyes were clear and not glazed over from the lingering effects of pain medication, I left my finger where it was even as Christopher dropped his hand. I knew I needed to say something, to do something that would break the spell we'd somehow both fallen under, but I kept my mouth shut. I'd been dreaming of getting a chance like this pretty much from the time I'd been reintroduced to Christopher, and I wasn't going to waste it.

His lips were as soft as I'd imagined but also smooth and supple. They were made for kissing.

Me.

They were made for kissing *me.*

A wave of possessiveness swept through me, consuming me. It wasn't like anything I'd ever felt before, even when I'd been dating other people. None of them had ever inspired my brain to play the same word on a loop like it was doing now.

Mine.

Christopher hadn't moved at all when I'd touched his mouth, but now as his eyes slid shut, he drew in a sharp breath and shifted his head enough so that my finger was precariously close to the middle of his slightly parted lips. I took him up on his silent invitation and let my finger slide over the center of his upper lip, then the lower one.

The need to taste him was like a living thing inside of me clawing to get out.

I probably could have kept it under wraps if Christopher hadn't decided to open his eyes at that exact moment and, more importantly, hadn't pressed his lips together and softly kissed my finger.

It was all the permission I needed.

Admittedly, I didn't give him a chance to change his mind. As I moved my hand so I could clasp his cheek, my mouth was already on his, swallowing his startled gasp.

His taste was like a drug. One hit of it and I knew I would always want more. He'd ruined me for anyone else, man or woman.

With one kiss.

I kissed him deeply and let my tongue slide over his in greeting. He let out a surprised sound and broke the kiss. Thankfully, I was able to rein in my raging lust to recognize the need for me to back off.

I began to straighten back into a sitting position so I could put some space between us, but Christopher grabbed the back of my neck with his uninjured hand and followed me until he was practically pressed against me.

"No, please, Rush—" Christopher began before he sucked in what seemed to be some needed air.

Fuck, had I scared him so badly that he couldn't breathe?

"Christopher—"

"I'm sorry, I can do better," Christopher interrupted. "Please, I just… please."

The desperation in his voice had me pausing long enough to recognize a couple of things. First off, his hold on the back of my neck almost bordered on painful. Second, he'd pressed his forehead against mine. And finally, his breaths were seesawing in and out of him.

Like mine.

He wanted this. He wanted it as much as I did.

Then why had he been surprised when I'd…

"Christopher, has no one ever—"

Before I could finish, Christopher released me and tried to put some space between us. If I hadn't closed a hand around his forearm, he would have probably been off the bed and gone. Every ounce of excitement had been sucked out of the room.

"Christopher—"

"I'm not a virgin," Christopher interrupted. His eyes were downcast, and I could practically feel the shame wafting off him. "He… he just never wanted to kiss me."

I tried to make sense of what he was saying. So he'd had sex before, but his partner hadn't kissed him on the mouth? How was that even possible? Unless it had been a random hookup. But I knew in my gut Christopher wasn't a random hookup kind of guy.

I must have been quiet for too long because Christopher tried to pull away from me. Instead of releasing him, I pulled him closer. Not surprisingly, he began to fight me, but I knew it was because he was embarrassed.

"Let go!" Christopher snapped impatiently.

I put my hand at the back of his neck and began rubbing my thumb back and forth over his soft skin. "Stop," I commanded as he continued to fight me. "Christopher, just stop," I repeated softly.

He did, but his entire body was wound up tight.

Ready to take advantage of any opportunity to escape.

I closed my eyes and pressed our foreheads together like they'd been before things had fallen apart. "Christopher, will you…" I began, but then a mass of nerves unfurled in my stomach. What if I lost him before I'd really had him?

To my surprise, Christopher was no longer trying to pull away. I pulled in a deep breath in an effort to get control of myself. I opened my eyes and pulled back enough to find Christopher watching me. He looked like he was trying to decide between staying or running.

"Christopher, will you let me be this first for you?"

I saw in his eyes the exact moment when he realized what I was asking. They went wide for a moment, then relaxed. His entire body softened in my hold until no part of him was resisting me. I slipped my free arm around his waist, pulling him in close so that our chests were nearly touching. I should have been relieved he was wearing a T-shirt and sweats and that I was fully dressed, but the lack of skin on skin irritated me. If this was the only chance I got to taste him, touch him, I didn't want to squander it.

But I needed to make this about Christopher. About what he needed, deserved.

Instead of covering Christopher's mouth again with mine, I leaned in and let my nose brush against his as I took in his scent.

"Oranges," I murmured as I lowered my mouth enough to kiss the left side of his mouth. "My favorite," I added as I trailed my mouth down Christopher's chin, then his throat.

Christopher tipped his head back to accommodate me. "I, um, usually get the—"

His words were replaced with a gasp as I closed my lips over his pulse point and sucked gently. It wasn't until I began retracing my path back to his mouth that I reminded him of what he'd been about to say. "You usually get the...?"

Both of Christopher's arms were now around my neck, and he was nearly straddling one of my thighs, so I could feel the little tremors that were snaking throughout his body.

"Huh?"

I let the arm I'd had around his waist drop enough so I could support his thigh. But it wasn't until I stopped kissing him that Christopher opened his eyes, which were mixed with disappointment and confusion.

"You usually get the...?" I prodded. His responses so far had proven what a passionate lover he'd be. To be so lost already after just a few touches... he wouldn't be able to hide anything from me when we made love.

The reasonable part of my brain reminded me to focus on the present, not on things that might never be. As strong as my feelings for Christopher were, there was still so much I didn't know about him, and I had no clue if he wanted me beyond a first kiss.

"Lemon," Christopher said impatiently. His uninjured hand cupped my cheek. "I usually buy the lemon bodywash, but the store was out. I... I can keep getting the orange," he said hesitantly.

I managed not to smile at his nervous declaration. Instead, I kissed the other side of his mouth. "Sweetheart, it doesn't matter what you buy," I said as I teased the crease where his lips met. "As long as it's on this beautiful body," I continued as I slid my hand up and down his slim thigh, "it's going to be my favorite."

Christopher went very still in my hold. His eyes met mine. He was blinking rapidly like he was trying to keep from crying.

"Don't say stuff like that, okay?"

It wasn't a command. It wasn't even a request. It was a plea.

An out-and-out plea that made me want to kill the man who'd hurt Christopher so badly.

"Which part?" I asked, though I already knew. "The part about you being beautiful or the insinuation that this won't be the only time we're together like this."

"Both," Christopher responded.

I could already feel him trying to mentally back away. I kept my hold on him firm as I leaned in and gently brushed my mouth over his. "Can't do that," I said before kissing him softly again. "I'm going to do everything in my power to make sure this happens again… and often." I drew out the next kiss and added a little lick to the seam of his mouth. His gasp almost made me forget my next words.

Almost, but not quite.

I made sure to put a little distance between our mouths so I could really look at him. As soon as Christopher's eyes opened and focused on me, I said, "Do you see that chair?"

I made sure to wait until he glanced at the rickety chair in the corner. When he nodded, I continued with "That's where I spent the whole night because I couldn't take my eyes off of you, Christopher. I can't take my hands off of you right now. You *are* beautiful, Christopher. So many kinds of beautiful. And if things go the way I want them to, I'll be able to spend the rest of my life proving it to you."

I didn't give him a chance to respond or myself too much time to acknowledge what I'd just basically admitted to. Instead, I got started on my promise and sealed my mouth over his.

CHAPTER EIGHT

CHRISTOPHER

+4

I was sure I would die under the onslaught of Rush's kiss and all the emotions that came with it. I still couldn't comprehend how I'd even woken up with the man sitting on my bed, his finger caressing my skin. I also couldn't fathom what I'd been thinking when I'd kissed his finger.

Except I *did* know what I'd been thinking, or hoping, rather.

This.

Exactly this.

I wanted to believe that his mouth had been made for mine because we seemed to fit together perfectly. And wherever he led, I followed. I had no idea if I was fumbling my first real kiss or not, but I didn't care.

That was what Rush did for me.

He kept the darkness at bay. The fear, the shame, the disappointment, none of those had a voice when Rush was touching me, when his mouth was feasting on mine. He was my only focus. Pleasing him, showing him how much he pleased me—that was now my only goal in life.

It didn't take long before I figured out how to return his kisses. It was such a natural thing that when Rush broke the kiss for a moment,

I took control of it. As I explored his mouth, the flames that had been simmering inside of me became a full-on inferno, and I soon found myself nearly straddling Rush's lower half.

My lesson in kissing quickly became something else entirely, and I wasn't sure which one of us had started it. All I knew was that in a matter of seconds, both of Rush's hands were gripping my ass through my sweats, and I had both my hands on his face as we kissed. When Rush pulled me forward, I could feel his hardness against my own, even through several layers of fabric.

"Rush," I whispered brokenly once I managed to rip my mouth from his. But I couldn't stop moving my hips as I instinctively searched for something. I felt like I was going to explode into a million pieces, and I both feared and wanted that.

"I've got you, baby," Rush responded, and then he used his hands on my ass to grind my hips against his. I cried out at how amazing it felt to have his hard cock sliding against mine. I had no control, no idea what to do next. I just had Rush and an intrinsic trust in him that he would take care of me.

With every thrust of his body against mine, there was a coil inside of me that began to grow tighter and tighter. So tight that I began to fear what would happen when it snapped. The logical side of me understood what was happening, but no amount of reading about this very thing in books could have prepared me for *this*. No amount of daydreaming about this exact moment when I'd been younger had readied me for what I was feeling, both physically and emotionally. And no attempt at self-pleasure could even scratch the surface of what was happening.

Rush continued to kiss me as he worked our bodies. I had no clue if he was experiencing any of the same sensations as me, but I was too far gone to care. I tore my mouth from his and buried my face in the crook of his neck.

"Rush," I said, though my voice didn't sound like my own.

Rush didn't say anything, but he didn't need to because he was giving me exactly what I needed. More speed, more power, more contact. He drove me straight to the edge of an invisible precipice. I was afraid he'd leave me hanging there, but he kept up the frenzied pace of our lower bodies grinding together. I could feel the powerful muscles of his back beneath my hands as I clung to him, and his breath came in heavy pants against my ear. But it wasn't until he whispered, "Come for me, sweetheart," that everything flew apart inside of me.

I cried out as I came. I dug my fingers into Rush's body as wave after wave of pleasure washed over me. The tears I'd been keeping at bay for months began to slip down my cheeks. Unfortunately, so did the emotions I'd been holding prisoner deep inside of me for just as long. As the natural high began to wind down, the despair, the loneliness, the stark terror of the unknown all came crashing down on me, and the silent tears turned to ugly sobs.

I tried to pull free of Rush's hold so I could escape in shame, but he refused to release me. At some point he'd moved one of his hands up to my back and the other to the back of my head. I was trapped whether I liked it or not. And deep down in the emptiness of my soul, I did like it. I couldn't deny it.

But I also couldn't let it happen. It would become this ugly, aching thing when it was taken away from me.

And it would be taken away.

Despite my struggles, Rush just hugged me tighter. But it was his words that ultimately did me in, that took the fight right out of me.

"Let go, Christopher. You're safe, sweetheart."

So that was exactly what I did.

It was ugly and uncontrollable, and while I tried more than once to get ahold of myself, the tears kept coming, the cries of rage and anguish didn't let up, and I clung to Rush like he was my lifeline.

Which he very much was, even if that hadn't been his intention.

I couldn't say how long my meltdown lasted, but by the time I was able to make sense of the present, I was wrung out. The powerful orgasm was nothing more than a memory now. I'd been shown the heights of pleasure for the first time and by a man I could only classify as perfect, and I'd turned it into my own personal pity party.

My mind began to race with what to say to Rush, or at least how to extricate my body from his, when a sharp sound suddenly pierced the silence.

Mission very much accomplished.

I jerked backward enough to put some space between me and Rush, but his hand at my back prevented me from escaping entirely.

"It's the secondary alarm on my phone," he said gently. "I was afraid I'd keep hitting snooze on the first one if I fell asleep, so I set a second one."

I barely managed to process his words because I was too busy memorizing every detail of his face. His hair was sticking up in several spots, probably thanks to my roaming fingers. His eyes were that nearly black color again, but his expression was soft and relaxed. His gorgeous lips looked as gently bruised as mine felt, proof of how perfectly and often our mouths had melded.

"You need to take your medicine."

Rush's words tore me from the haze I'd been in. "What?" I asked in surprise.

"That's why I set the alarm. Dr. Kleinman told me to make sure you take your medicines at the right times."

Right.

Because I was sick.

Used.

Dirty.

Pain slashed through me as the pieces clicked into place. He'd driven me to Dr. Kleinman's office because of my hand, and he'd stayed the night because they'd given me something for the pain. Dr. Kleinman had made him feel obligated to stay.

So all that talk about how beautiful I was while I slept…

I shook my head in disbelief as I realized I'd repeated the same mistakes that had left me in the position I was in.

They'd just been pretty words, probably spoken out of pity, especially after I'd instigated the whole thing by kissing his finger.

As my mind began to replay the events of the last twenty-four hours at a rapid rate, his words from the day before hit me like a ton of bricks. He'd said them just before I'd fallen asleep in the car. I'd asked him if he'd ever found love. Despite being half-asleep, I still remembered how the words had cut through me.

Not yet. But I think all of that is about to change.

He was with someone. Someone important. Someone he was falling in love with. How had I forgotten that?

"Christopher?"

Rush's confusion was clear. Probably because I was still practically sitting on his lap.

"Sorry," I muttered and made a move to climb off him, but his hands closed around my hips. Startled, I lifted my eyes to meet his.

"What just happened?" Rush asked.

"Nothing," I murmured. "You're right, it's time to take my medicine."

I made another move to extricate myself from his hold, but he wouldn't release me. His eyes had gone from soft to hard just like that, and like when I'd first met him, I couldn't tell what he was thinking.

It was unnerving as hell.

Especially since he wasn't letting me go so we could just pretend the whole thing hadn't happened.

"What just happened, Christopher?" Rush repeated, his voice a hell of a lot sterner this time around.

My response was the usual one.

Escape.

Just escape.

"Let go," I ordered because anger and escape worked better together.

"Not until you tell me what the fuck happened in the last two minutes. I'm going to need a little bit more explanation as to why I went from having the best orgasm of my entire life followed by a level of intimacy I've never known with anyone to you wanting to get as far away from me as you can," Rush bit out.

I stilled at his words. He'd come too? I automatically looked down at his lap.

"Need proof?" Rush asked angrily.

He grabbed my uninjured hand and settled it on his jeans. His *damp* jeans.

Lies. Just lies, the insidious voice in my head whispered. *Like Peter's.*

Desperation had me shoving both hands hard against Rush's chest. He finally released his hold on my hips but only so he could grab my wrists instead. I climbed off him and prepared to fight to make him release me.

"Just wait, Christopher. Make sure you're steady on your feet first," Rush said. It was then that I realized he wasn't holding on to my wrists with much force. If anything, he was acting as a physical support to keep me from losing my balance.

Which I nearly did because my legs felt like noodles.

"I'm good," I said after a minute because I really needed to put some distance between him and me.

A strange stand-off began as we stared at one another. But while I was wary and waiting for him to try and grab me again, Rush just looked… disappointed. After several beats, Rush dropped his eyes and ran his palms over his thighs.

Like he needed to get something off his hands.

Something like me.

"Your medications are on the nightstand. The prescription for the pain meds is the one in the blue bottle. Dr. Kleinman said to take one every four to six hours as needed for pain."

With that, Rush got up and began leaving the room.

Exactly like I wanted.

So then why did it hurt so fucking much?

"Don't worry, I'm not going to tell anyone. Your friend won't find out," I called just as he reached the bedroom door.

Rush stopped, but he didn't answer me, nor did he turn around. A strange sense of panic came over me, but it had nothing to do with my next statement.

"I'd appreciate it if you didn't tell anyone in my family about any of this," I managed to get out.

I instantly knew I'd gone too far when I saw Rush's muscles go tight. When he slowly turned around and stalked toward me, I was scared.

Not that he'd physically hurt me because I knew in my heart he wasn't capable of something like that. I was scared that I'd fucked up.

Really fucked up.

The mere fact that he hadn't just continued out of the room was proof that I'd pushed him too far.

I managed to stand my ground, but that was mostly because with the nightstand just a couple of feet behind me, there wasn't really anywhere to go.

Rush stopped several feet from me. His eyes weren't cold and emotionless like I expected. They burned with anger.

Anger and something else.

Something I didn't have the guts to give a name to.

"First off," Rush began. "What and when you decide to tell your family is your business and yours alone. If you'd given me even half a chance, I would have proven to you that I was a man of my word. That goes for everything I said and did this morning too. If you wanted a pity fuck, that wasn't it," Rush snapped as he pointed at the bed. "I'm not saying I'm a saint, but I don't fuck around with people's heads to get what I want. And I sure as shit don't expose my throat to them like that." He again pointed at the bed.

Rush fell silent and half turned around like he was going to leave. He took his time turning around. This time, the anger was gone, and in its place was the emotion I hadn't recognized before.

Hurt.

A whole hell of a lot of hurt.

"I can only assume by your comment about not telling my 'friend' that you're under the misconception that I'm in a relationship with someone. Something else you would have eventually learned about me is that I don't fuck around when I'm seeing someone."

Rush turned and headed back toward the bedroom door. I pounced on the obvious lie he'd just uttered and said, "So I guess I just imagined what you said to me yesterday in the car about not having fallen in love yet but that all of that was about to change. Did I miss the part where you fell out of love and dumped your partner in the handful of hours that I was asleep? I'm not stupid, Rush."

Rush paused. "No, no you're not. You just can't see the truth even when it's right in front of you."

Frustration consumed me along with a hefty dose of doubt as Rush reached for the doorknob.

"I don't understand!" I practically shouted. "You said you were falling in love. I saw the way you smiled right before you said it. Why won't you just admit it?"

"Admit what?" Rush shouted back as he turned around but this time, he didn't move toward me. "That I'm the stupid one for falling for someone who will never trust me because some fucker from his past hurt him too badly? That I'm the idiot for losing my heart to someone who will never accept what's standing right in front of him?" Rush paused and ran his fingers through his hair. "I was talking about you, Christopher! In that fucking car yesterday… I was talking about you."

I shook my head in disbelief, but there wasn't a chance of me speaking because my throat had closed up tight.

Rush let out a sigh and then took in a few deep breaths, apparently trying to calm himself. When he did speak, his voice was quieter but no less passionate.

"As much as I want to hide and lick my wounds, I'm not going to. Not if there's even a scintilla of a chance of getting everything I've ever wanted. The only way you're getting me out of your life is if you can honestly look me in the eye and tell me you don't feel even a fraction of what I feel for you. I won't take anything less than that, Christopher."

With that, Rush threw open the door and left the room. He didn't even slam the door behind him. He just closed it, and that was it.

I was alone again. Even the ugly voice that had been stripping away pieces of my soul for the past six months was gone.

There was just… nothing.

CHAPTER NINE

RUSH

74

Admittedly, it wasn't my finest hour. Or thirty minutes, rather, since that was how long it took before I heard footsteps on the stairs. In the time since I'd left the bedroom until I'd heard that first step, I'd been trying to keep myself busy so I wouldn't return the room and demand that Christopher admit that what had happened between us was real and that he'd felt it too. A former boyfriend had once told me our breakup had left him gutted, but I hadn't truly understood what he'd meant until this moment. I felt like someone had carved my insides out with a spoon, leaving behind my painfully pounding heart and a whole lot of nothing else.

How had I let this happen? Two days ago, I'd literally been standing in this same kitchen (minus the cooling cum in my shorts) living what I'd thought was a fulfilled life. Aside from the loss of my parents, I'd been enjoying what I'd been given. I loved my job, I'd been excited to move to a new city where I'd be closer to my friend and hopefully become a part of his large, extended family. My biggest worry had been trying to find a house with a big enough yard for my floppy-eared brood to roam when not snuggled up in the spacious rabbit mansion I was planning on building them.

Now life seemed like it was on hold and I had no control over anything. I'd wanted what my parents had had, but it had never occurred to me that I could lose my heart to someone who either didn't feel the same thing or who bore too many emotional scars that couldn't be overcome.

Once I'd realized that it wasn't just attraction I was feeling for the troubled young man from four years earlier, my plan had been to take things slowly.

Turtle speed at most.

Crazily enough, twenty-four hours ago, my biggest concerns hadn't had anything to do with getting past Christopher's obvious walls. I'd been more worried about King's reaction to my interest in his nephew.

Now, a mere day later, I'd learned Christopher's biggest secret, given him his first kiss, and shared an explosive orgasm with him all before exposing my emotional jugular. I'd never told anyone I was with in the past that I'd loved them because I hadn't. It was something I'd known I would need to be one hundred percent certain of before I said the words. Yet half an hour ago, I'd pretty much said them to a young man who, for all intents and purposes, had only just met me and who wasn't in any position to deal with the admission.

"Fuck," I muttered to myself as I got the burner going again. Once I heard the floor creak slightly near the kitchen entryway, I said, "I didn't know what kind of eggs you liked, but the bacon's done, so it will just take a few minutes depending on how you want them. Even if you're not hungry, you need to eat. Those meds aren't—"

Before I could finish my sentence, a pair of long, slim arms wrapped around me from behind. I was shocked into silence as Christopher pressed his head between my shoulder blades and settled his hands over my heart.

"Sorry," he whispered, and then, just like that, he was gone. But not far. He was pulling plates out of one of the cabinets.

Two plates.

"I like them over easy," Christopher said softly.

I didn't know what to make of any of it, but it sure did feel like a victory. I'd take it. I'd take any win with him that I could get.

By the time the food was done, Christopher had set places at the island for both of us. I was glad I'd had the foresight to clear the boxes off them during my mini cleaning of the kitchen.

Not a word was spoken as we ate, and Christopher mostly kept his eyes down, but I was okay with that. I could tell he was nervous, and if minimizing eye contact helped him relax, then so be it.

A soft meow caught my attention. Pip was trying to put his claws into my jeans, presumably so he could crawl up the fabric, but he couldn't manage to hold his balance long enough. I leaned down and scooped him up, then stood and took him to the other side of the island and handed him to Christopher. I figured the kitten would soothe Christopher in a way that little else could. As both man and mini beast got comfortable, I began clearing the table. It was only when I turned my back to Christopher and began washing the dishes that I finally heard him speak.

"Did Uncle King tell you what happened the night he and I met for the first time?" Christopher carefully asked.

"Only that a guy was attacking you, but your uncle intervened and told you to take your sister and run."

I glanced over my shoulder to see that Christopher had his eyes glued to his cat. I forced myself to keep working on the dishes.

"His name was Barry. My mom's boyfriend, Ricky, used to pimp Uncle Micah out to men for drug money. I don't know exactly how old Uncle Micah was, but he was still a kid. A kid raising kids."

"He protected you," I suggested. I'd given up on trying to finish the dishes. It didn't seem to matter since Christopher was speaking freely.

"He did," Christopher agreed. "He took Ricky's beatings upon himself, he made sure me and Rory didn't see all the stuff that went on in that house… the drugs, our mom prostituting herself. Uncle Micah gave us as normal a life as he could."

"He loved you and your sister very much," I said as I returned to my seat. Christopher had yet to look at me, but I didn't care. I just needed him to keep talking.

"More than anything," Christopher responded. He was silent for a really long time, the only proof that he was still caught up in the past being a single tear slipping down his face and landing on Pip's fur.

"As I got older, I started to understand what was happening. The back room, all the men..." Christopher shook his head. "I never tried to help him. Not when Ricky was beating the shit out of him, not when he was being dragged to that back room. I just got under the covers with Rory and covered her ears so she wouldn't hear any of it. When Micah came back to the room, I'd pretend to be asleep because I was too ashamed to face him. I was such a fucking coward."

I opened my mouth to protest, but Christopher cut me off by saying, "Please Rush, I just need to get this out, okay?"

It went against my nature to let anyone, let alone the man I was losing my heart to, suffer through something on their own, but I knew Christopher was right. He wasn't looking for platitudes about how he'd done the best he could. He just needed to purge all the ugliness inside of him.

"Okay," I responded.

"One day, Ricky came and picked me up from school. I usually stayed in the library after classes were done and studied until Uncle Micah and Rory came to get me. Uncle Micah had told me to never leave the school without him and to never go home alone. Ricky didn't give me any choice in the matter. He just grabbed my arm and pulled me to his car. I didn't understand what was happening until Ricky led me to my bedroom, the one I shared with Micah and Rory. He told me to sit down on the bed, and then this guy, Barry, came in. Barry... Barry was one of the regulars who... who hurt Uncle Micah."

I could feel the rage simmering through my veins, but I tamped it down. I already knew from King that Christopher had ultimately escaped the assault, but that didn't mean he hadn't been traumatized.

"After Barry paid Ricky and Ricky left, Barry sat on the bed next to me and began to touch me... and himself. I couldn't move. I couldn't speak. I couldn't do anything. Even when Barry talked about Uncle Micah and the sick things he did to him, I didn't do anything because I was so fucking scared," Christopher explained. His voice had dropped considerably, so it was hard to hear him, but his body language spoke volumes. He was hunched over like he was trying to fold his body in on itself to make himself as small a target as he could.

"He was going to fuck me up against the wall. I can still feel the coldness of it against my cheek. I can still smell him as he held me there and told me I was going to be his special boy. I didn't move, not even when he released me so he could drop his pants. I could have pushed him and made a run for it, but I didn't. I didn't tell him to stop, I didn't struggle when he began unbuttoning my jeans. I'm not sure I even cried. I just accepted it. When Uncle Micah showed up, he tore Barry away from me and told me to take Rory and run. I didn't once think about staying behind to help him fight off Barry or Ricky. I ran. I just ran."

"What do you think would have happened to your sister if you hadn't run?" I asked.

Christopher merely shrugged.

"King told me what happened when he went after you and your sister that night. He said you found a spot to hide where he had no way of reaching you and that you kept your body between him and Rory the whole time."

There was still no real response from Christopher, and I knew anything else I said would just fall on deaf ears. Christopher had developed his narrative a long time ago, and no amount of me telling him he'd done exactly the right thing was going to change that.

At least not today.

Over time? Maybe.

"Uncle Micah saved me that night, and four years ago, you did the same thing," Christopher said. He finally looked at me. "My very own knight in shining armor," he said, though the words were hollow. He dropped his eyes to Pip again. "I didn't fight that night either. Not when the guys grabbed us and not when the one took me into that room. Gio, he tried to take them all on. Maybe if I'd helped... but surprise, surprise, I was too scared... again."

"I saw the tail end of that fight, Christopher. You guys were outnumbered and outmatched. And you *did* fight. I saw you try to go for that fire alarm. You used your head to try and find a way out of the situation. Just like you used your head when you hid from King in a spot where you knew he wouldn't be able to reach you."

Christopher didn't respond. I let out a sigh because I'd done exactly what I'd told myself I wouldn't. "I'm sorry," I said, daring to reach across the island to briefly touch Christopher's forearm. The fact that he didn't pull away from me was something at least.

"I was so grateful for you that night, Rush. So grateful," Christopher said softly. He looked at me, and I could see tears pooling in his eyes. He angrily dashed at what was clearly an unwanted show of emotion. He dropped his eyes again and added, "But I knew I wouldn't be lucky enough to get a third time."

I was about to ask him what he meant when he said, "I knew I wouldn't be able to stop someone if they…" He paused briefly before continuing. "What if it happened while I was on a date? What if someone grabbed me from off the street and pulled me into an alley? Con had taught me some self-defense moves before that night in the club, but I didn't use any of them. I knew I wouldn't use them in those other situations either. So I made a decision that night, in that room that I should have been raped in."

My heart hurt for Christopher. The terror in his voice was so strong that the attack at the club might as well have happened yesterday.

"What was the decision?" I asked.

"Since I couldn't protect myself, I'd have to make sure I was never in a situation where someone could hurt me like that. So that's what I did."

As unreasonable as his argument sounded, I also knew how desperate and vulnerable Christopher had to have been feeling after escaping not one, but two violent sexual assaults.

"How?" I asked.

"It was easy. I finished my last year of high school online. I never went anywhere by myself, and the only events I went to were ones where I knew that only people I trusted would be there. I spent most days studying and reading."

"But not the romance novels," I offered.

Christopher shook his head sharply. "They made me want something I knew I could never have."

"Love?" I suggested.

"A happily ever after," Christopher responded. "I couldn't risk dropping my guard, and I knew that reading those books would cause me to do exactly that, especially once I got to college."

"What about your undergraduate work here in Seattle?"

Christopher shrugged. "It was pretty much the same as high school. I did as much work as I could online. I only left my dorm to go to classes. Uncle Micah or Con would pick me up to go grocery shopping so that I wouldn't have to eat in the cafeteria."

"What happened when you left home for school in North Carolina?"

"I kept doing everything I'd been doing. I got my own dorm room instead of sharing, I scheduled my classes for during the day so the campus would be busy when I walked to class, I ordered groceries online and only ate in my room. I didn't participate in any activities, I didn't go to parties, I never left my room after it got dark, and I became hyperaware of my surroundings." Christopher paused before adding, "It became like this twenty-four-hour-a-day, seven-day-a-week job."

"That kind of life couldn't have been sustainable," I said. I was horrified at the prospect of the sweet, smart, kindhearted Christopher locking himself away from the world.

"I needed it to be," Christopher responded. "I figured I'd eventually get to a point where I felt more comfortable with the campus and the other students in my nursing program, but things got worse. By the end of my first semester, I was borderline agoraphobic. I'd stopped sleeping because I was convinced someone would come into my room. I was lying to my family about everything, and I'd stopped going home, even for holidays and the summer. I told everyone I was taking extra courses. Uncle Micah and Con came to visit a couple of times, and I managed to convince them I was loving college life each time. I was able to keep my grades up with no problem, but the stress was starting to make me sick. It was hard to keep food down, and after a while, I just wasn't hungry. I couldn't hide my appearance from my family, so I just cut off contact more and more. I blamed it all on school and studying. Last fall when I started the second semester of the program, I tried to start taking better care of myself. The curriculum included classes with a lot more hands-on training, which meant working with patients and shadowing other nurses."

"How did you do it?" I asked. I was still trying to make sense of the isolated life Christopher had forced himself into.

"It was hard at first, but having a routine helped. Most of the other students in the program were women, so it was easier to be around them. Several of them lived in my dorm, so I would walk to and from the hospital with them, and it didn't take long for them to start inviting me to things like coffee after class, study sessions, stuff like that. I hadn't really realized how lonely I'd become until I started hanging out with them."

"What happened?" I asked after several minutes of Christopher going silent. He looked tired. Instead of prodding him to respond, I stood up and went around the island. I held out my hand and waited.

It took Christopher a painfully long time to make a move. When he finally did, I let out a sigh of relief. Christopher tucked Pip in the crook of his right arm and took my hand with his left one. Neither of us spoke as I led him up the stairs to his room. When I pulled the covers back off the bed, toed my shoes off, and then got in it, I fully expected Christopher to panic. But to my surprise, he crawled in next to me. When I urged him into my arms so he could rest his head on my chest, he did it without hesitation. Pip ended up on my chest too, though he had Christopher's hand to support him so he wouldn't topple off during his nap.

"His name was Peter," Christopher began on his own. "He trans-ferred into the program a few weeks into the second semester. The girls I hung out with immediately accepted him into their circle. Our circle, I guess. I told myself I needed to keep my distance from the group, but I really didn't want to. It felt like the group was the only normal thing in my life. Peter wasn't a big guy or anything, so I guess that helped. It was clear that he was gay early on because he'd talk to the girls about his past boyfriends. He was pretty much an open book, and he seemed to know that I needed him to keep his distance. Eventually I started to feel safe enough to participate in the conversations, but I made sure I was never in a situation where I was alone with him."

"But something changed," I said. As much as I loved the feel of Christopher's weight on my chest, I couldn't really enjoy it because I knew what was coming.

Christopher nodded. "It was right before the holiday break. We were meeting up before everyone went home for Christmas. It ended up being a setup."

"A setup?" I asked in confusion.

"Yeah, um, the girls made it so Peter and I were left alone for the coffee date. They'd decided to play matchmaker, and each one texted excuses for why they couldn't come for coffee that day after Peter and I were already there. When I realized what they'd done, I started to panic, but Peter was the one to call the whole thing off. He apologized to me because even though he really liked me, he was still trying get over his breakup with his last boyfriend."

"So he supposedly took the chance of you guys getting together off the table," I said.

"And I fell for it hook, line, and sinker," Christopher murmured. "I'd always been better at listening than talking when I was younger, so it was easy to be a sympathetic ear. His boyfriend had cheated on him back in Ohio where they'd both grown up, so Peter had decided not to go home for the holidays so he wouldn't end up running into him. When he found out I wasn't going home either, Peter suggested we keep meeting for coffee. But he didn't push, and when I turned down his offer to walk me home, he didn't seem bothered by it. So we met up each day and even found a Chinese restaurant near campus that was open on Christmas Day."

Christopher fell silent for a long time. "He was so easy to talk to. I don't even really know when things changed. There was just this one day that I needed to tell him about the attacks. I didn't know why. I hadn't talked to anyone about them before, but I felt like there was this heavy weight on my chest and I couldn't breathe anymore because of it. He actually cried for me. We started spending more and more time together after that, and a couple months into the second semester, he told me he loved me. We hadn't done much more than hold hands at that point. He said he wanted to take things slow for me. He'd kiss me on the cheek or the forehead but never on the mouth. I didn't really understand why, but I didn't want to risk losing him, so I never asked him. Looking back, there were other warning signs that something wasn't quite right."

"Like what?" I asked. I was running my fingers through Christopher's hair at the same time that he was tapping one of his fingers softly on my chest. It took me a while to realize he was timing the tap to my heartbeat.

"He'd blow up at me sometimes for no reason at all. He'd disappear for a week or two at a time claiming he was sick, but he wouldn't let me see him. His physical appearance changed too. He looked more and more run-down, and he'd often lose track of a conversation. I once saw some concealer on his chin, but when I asked him about it, he flipped out."

"Did he ever hit you?" I asked.

Christopher shook his head. "After the concealer thing, he told me he was covering up a couple of bruises from some guys who'd knocked him around because he was gay."

I stiffened when I realized what Christopher wasn't saying. I actually sat up a little, forcing Christopher to shift his position. He ended up sitting cross-legged on the bed alongside my hip.

"Being gone for weeks at a time because he was sick… concealer on his face…?" I shook my head in disbelief. "He knew he had AIDS."

I hadn't been able to keep the rage out of my voice. Christopher dropped his eyes and began winding his fingers together.

"Fuck, I'm sorry," I murmured as I sat up even more, picking up Pip in the process. I handed the miffed kitten to Christopher.

"I wasn't smart enough to put it together," Christopher said after a few moments. "My feelings for him had started to get stronger, but I was nervous about having sex with him. He finally wore me down one afternoon while we were in my dorm room studying. It started off innocently enough with just some light touching and teasing. He told me how much he loved me and that he just wanted to be with me. I agreed but asked him to go slow and told him he had to wear a condom. He agreed. He even made a big show of putting it on so I could see. When he got behind me and started to push inside, it hurt a lot. All I felt was the burn. I thought it would get better if Peter just gave me some time to adjust, but as soon as he was inside of me, it was like something changed. He was rough and angry and at one point he even called me his ex's name. It was over in minutes. When he was done, he said it had been fun and began pulling on his clothes. I could... I could..."

The shell that Christopher had cloaked himself in from the moment he'd started speaking began to crack. His voice was no longer even and disinterested, and he'd started to rock his body back and forth.

"Take your time, sweetheart," I said as I shifted closer to him. I put my legs on either side of him so that I could pull him against my chest.

"I could feel something coming out of me. I thought it was blood. I thought maybe he'd torn something inside of me."

"But it wasn't blood," I said softly. It took every ounce of energy I had to keep my voice calm and my grip on Christopher gentle.

"No, it wasn't. Peter was still getting dressed, so I confronted him with it. He just smiled and said condoms sometimes broke. That smile... it made everything inside of me cold," Christopher admitted. "I found the condom on the floor next to the bed. There was nothing in it, and there weren't any tears, not big enough ones anyway for that amount of semen to pass through it."

"What did you do?" I asked.

Christopher shook his head. "I don't really remember. I showered. I know that. But everything else is a blur."

"Did you go to the authorities?"

Christopher laughed harshly. "And tell them what? I'd had sex with my boyfriend, but I'd been too stupid to realize he'd taken the condom off at some point?"

"You are not stupid," I said angrily as I forced Christopher to look at me. "And you are not at fault in any of this. You trusted him to protect you. You trusted him to take care of you. You were inexperienced and in pain, so what baseline did you have to tell you something was off when he put himself inside of you. You did everything right, Christopher."

Tears began to shimmer in Christopher's eyes, and I could only pray I wasn't the cause. I dragged him back against my chest. I held him like that for a long time until we'd both calmed down a bit. Pip had wandered off in the meantime, but not far. He was curled up in the middle of one of the pillows.

"Did you go get tested right away?" I asked.

"No," Christopher said. "I just wanted to forget about the whole thing. Honestly, it didn't even occur to me to get tested. I just wrote it off as Peter being someone who liked fucking guys bare and didn't have a problem using subterfuge to get what he wanted. He disappeared from the program a few days later. No one knew where he'd gone. A little over six months ago as I was nearing the end of the program, I shadowed a nurse who did hospice care. She'd go to different homes in the area to check on terminal patients who wanted to pass away at home rather than in a hospital or nursing home. Our last stop was this huge house a few miles from the university. The patient had AIDS and wasn't expected to last more than a week."

Christopher began to rock again despite being in my arms, so I took over and rocked both of us in the hopes it would help him get through the rest of his story.

"I couldn't make sense of what I was looking at. I didn't recognize him. Even when the nurse greeted him, I had no idea what was happening. It was like a wire between my eyes and brain had gotten cut. But *he* recognized *me*. He asked the nurse to get him some juice from the kitchen. Once she was gone, Peter started to laugh. He thought he'd missed his chance to see my expression when I found out. Turned out he liked telling the guys he fucked that he was positive, but he always waited a couple of months to give the disease time to progress. Said it was like fucking them all over again. But he'd gotten too sick before he could tell me. Turned out he'd infected over a dozen guys on purpose. He hadn't lied about having a boyfriend who'd cheated on him. That's how Peter got it. The boyfriend died within a month of learning he had it, and Peter figured he didn't have much time either, so why not take as many guys with him as he could. Didn't hurt if they also happened to look like his boyfriend."

"Jesus," I breathed.

We were still rocking back and forth, but I had a feeling I was the one who needed it at the moment. I'd never felt such a bone-chilling need to hurt someone. Despite what I did for a living, I wasn't a violent guy. But the knowledge that the fucker had put Christopher through all of this out of some sense of twisted revenge made me want to tear anything and everything around me to shreds. Christopher must have sensed my agitation because he sought out one of my hands and linked our fingers.

"Rush," Christopher said softly. "You can take them back… the things you said this morning. It's okay, really. I… I need you to take them back."

His request caught me off guard. Was he trying to give me an out? Did he really think anything he'd said had changed how I felt about him?

"Why?" I asked carefully.

He didn't answer at first. For a while I thought he wouldn't. But when he did finally speak, his words dropped me right between heaven and hell.

"Because I can't do it. I can't look you in the eye and tell you what happened this morning wasn't real. So I need you to do it. I need you to be the strong one."

CHAPTER TEN

CHRISTOPHER

44

It took a while for the fog of sleep to lift, which was a strange thing for me, probably because I didn't sleep well to begin with. But something about the softness of my bed felt different this morning. I could hear birds chirping, and a soft, cool breeze tickled my feet where they were sticking out from beneath the bedding. Any other morning, I probably would have enjoyed it.

No, that wasn't true.

I never opened the windows or drew back the curtains. I liked the darkness... it kept me grounded.

It keeps you from thinking about everything you're going to leave behind...

I sighed and rolled on my back but didn't make any effort to get up and shut the window or pull the curtains shut. My mind was already on the man who'd opened them in the first place.

I hadn't expected him to stay. I hadn't *wanted* him to stay because he would have just ended up being like the sunlight or the birds or the breeze.

Something I couldn't have.

Not while I didn't know what my future held.

I still couldn't believe I'd told Rush everything.

Everything.

I'd even admitted that I was beginning to feel something for the older man. Something I'd been fantasizing about for a long time. In the days and weeks after the attack in the club, Rush had occupied a lot of real estate in my head. A lot more than he should have. I'd always attributed my feelings to hero worship, but from the moment I'd opened the door and literally seen the man of my dreams standing next to my uncle on my front porch, that dark place where I'd forced those memories to live over the past few years had lit up like embers. I'd tried to snuff them back out after Rush had left, but it hadn't worked, and in the twenty-four hours since Rush had shown up on my doorstep a second time, every word he'd said, every touch of his fingers, had fueled those embers. And then his admission that he had feelings for me... well, those little embers had turned into a full-on inferno that I had no hope of coming back from.

I sighed and pulled in a deep breath, which served only to draw in Rush's faint scent.

He hadn't left the day before when I'd asked him to. He hadn't left last night either.

I'd been glad for both, though I couldn't have told him that. We'd ended up taking a nap together after breakfast. Around lunchtime, he'd woken me up much like he had that morning... with gentle caresses on my face, arms, and hands. They hadn't been sexual in nature, but I hadn't really known what to call them. It'd almost felt like he was reassuring himself that I was still there.

He'd made sandwiches for lunch, which we'd eaten in bed. We'd talked, but there'd been no mention of feelings or the past or future. Rush had simply asked me questions like what the most disgusting thing I'd ever eaten was and the best costume I'd ever worn for Halloween. My answer of Batman had been a game changer.

Rush was Team DC Comics.

Like me.

We'd spent the rest of the afternoon talking about the characters and exploring my vintage comic book collection that Rush had had to dig out of one of my many book boxes on the main floor of the house.

Then the movie marathon had started. We'd stopped long enough to order a pizza and then we'd spent the next several hours with various members of the Justice League. I'd loved every moment of it, especially since I'd gotten to do it all from the safety of Rush's embrace. I'd ended up falling asleep between movies, waking up only once during the night to find the TV off and Rush out cold with me sprawled on top of his chest and Pip asleep on his shoulder.

Both of Rush's arms had been around me.

It had been heaven.

This morning meant it was time to come back down to earth. I'd already told the insurance company I processed claims for that I'd be off for a couple of days because of my hand, so I wasn't really sure what to do with myself. I just knew I couldn't do something that involved my bed... like staying in it all day and feeling sorry for myself.

Not after the things that Rush had done to me in it.

My eyes automatically shifted to the spot where Rush had given me my first kiss, then my first real orgasm. But it was the moment right after that... the one where Rush had held me and just let me purge all the fear, guilt, and shame that continued to linger.

All of that was over now. He'd done as I'd asked. He'd been the strong one and walked away.

I sighed and forced myself to sit up. My eyes fell on the open window. There wasn't a cloud in the sky. It would be one of Seattle's rare, perfect days. When I'd been younger, Con and Micah would insist on getting out and enjoying everything the Pacific Northwest had to offer.

It'd been the best time of my life.

The reminder of my family and how I'd been pushing them away for so long made all the lightness I'd been feeling disintegrate, and instead of climbing to my feet like I'd been planning, I lay back down. The alarm on my watch began to chime, indicating it was time to take my medication.

For a brief moment, I wondered what it would be like if I didn't. I was fighting a battle where I had no idea what the outcome would be.

But if I accepted the outcome, I'd been battling for months now, there'd be no more not knowing. There'd be no more waiting and praying for numbers to go down. I'd be able to spend time with my family without any of it hanging over their heads until the very end when my condition would be impossible to hide.

I shook my head. I'd come this far. I'd see it through, and in a couple of months, I'd know which path my life would take.

I just needed to hold out a little longer.

I sighed and reached for my medications on the nightstand. That was when I noticed a bottle of water sitting next to the pill bottles and a small folded-over piece of paper with my name on it.

The goodbye note.

The one that said he was giving me what I wanted; he was walking away.

"Fuck," I whispered as tears pricked the backs of my eyes. I didn't want to read the thing. I wanted to ball it up and throw it out the stupid window so the perfect breeze could steal it away and take every moment of the last forty-eight hours with it.

But my fingers had different ideas. I opened the note and looked for the "Dear Christopher" part, but to my surprise, there was only a handful of words scrawled on the paper.

You might want to cover your ears.

"Wha—?" I began right before there was a booming sound downstairs. It was quickly followed by another, then another. I scrambled to my feet and hurried down the stairs.

"Hold up!" Rush called as soon as I reached the bottom step. "You need shoes and goggles."

Huh?

I looked around as best as I could from my position on the step. There were little bits of drywall here and there along with a lot of drywall dust. A glance at the living room showed the furniture had been covered in plastic. The antique side table was also carefully covered.

Rush appeared from the kitchen area with goggles on his face and a huge sledgehammer in his hand.

He was taking down my wall. The one I'd tried to do on my own.

When he reached me, Rush removed the goggles, and then he was dropping a kiss to my mouth. It was soft and sweet and over way too fast. "Morning," he said softly.

"Morning," I managed to respond.

"Put some shoes on before you come down. Did you take your medicine?"

"Um, no, but I was about to," I said.

"I made breakfast sandwiches. I'll put them in the oven to warm up while you get dressed, okay?"

I nodded dumbly. The question I should have been asking him never made it to my lips.

What are you still doing here?

I hurried back up the stairs to get dressed. It wasn't until I was fully dressed and reaching for my medication bottles that I realized what the strange, restless sensation in my chest was.

I was giddy.

I sat down in disbelief.

I was fucking giddy.

I was so happy that Rush was still here that I was speeding through everything to get back to him. What was that about? I was supposed to be trying to figure out a way to send him on his way.

He didn't leave.

I almost cried as my old voice pointed that fact out. I wiped at my eyes because I couldn't go where that voice wanted me to go. I couldn't start dreaming about Rush touching me again, kissing me again, saying those words he'd said the day before that I still wanted so badly to believe.

You are *beautiful, Christopher. So many kinds of beautiful. And if things go the way I want them to, I'll be able to spend the rest of my life proving it to you.*

I shook my head. I couldn't do this. I couldn't. I wouldn't. I had a plan to stick to, and Rush wasn't part of it. No one was. Just me. I'd brought all this upon myself with my stupidity, and I was the one who had to pay for it.

Me.

Just me.

"Christopher, food's ready!" I heard Rush call.

I needed to tell him I wasn't feeling well and that I was going to lie down. He'd stop taking down my wall, he'd leave breakfast for me to eat later, and he'd leave me alone to get some rest. I'd have the time I needed to shore up my defenses.

Yeah, that was what I would do.

"Coffee or juice or both?" Rush shouted. "Never mind, I'll do both!"

I smiled to myself when I heard him let out a curse right before the fire alarm went off.

"Extinguisher is under the sink!" I yelled even as a fit of laughter threatened to consume me. I quickly downed the rest of my pills and hurried down the stairs. The acrid smell of smoke hit me long before I reached the kitchen.

"Everything okay down here?" I asked. Rush had his back to me and appeared to be stirring something in a mixing bowl. He was wearing different clothes from the day before. His jeans were a little darker, and he had on a dark blue T-shirt. There was a sheen of smoke in the air around him, but I barely noticed. I was too busy drooling over his tattooed biceps.

"All good," he said as he turned around. "How many pancakes do you want?"

I managed to tear my eyes away, but when Rush gave me a little wink, I knew he'd caught me ogling his yummy body.

"What happened to the breakfast sandwiches?" I asked with a raise of my brow. The question put me back on more even ground. I swore I saw Rush's cheeks actually turn a bit pink.

"Oh, um," Rush began as he glanced at the sink, which had what looked like a cookie sheet sticking out of it. "Too many trans fats in them."

"Trans fats?"

Rush nodded. "That shit will kill you."

"Isn't that why the US banned the use of it in most foods a couple years back?" I asked.

Rush paused for a moment and then set the bowl down on the island. It was then that I noticed two places were already set.

I lifted my eyes only to nearly swallow my tongue with the way Rush was watching me. He looked like he wanted *me* for breakfast.

Yes, please.

I held my breath as he came around the island and closed the distance between us. I fully expected him to kiss me, but when his chest brushed mine, he didn't drop his head to take my mouth. Instead, he reached past me, and I realized he'd only been attempting to get to the counter behind me.

I felt like a fool and took a step back. I dropped my eyes in embarrassment because Rush had probably known what I'd been expecting.

But leave it to Rush to do the unexpected because not more than a couple seconds later, something soft brushed my lips and then my nose.

"Leave it to me to go crazy for a guy who's both a hottie *and* a smartie," Rush said softly as the scent of roses tickled my senses.

I opened my eyes and took in the sight of the most perfect rose I'd ever seen. It wasn't red though. It was a beautiful shade of light purple that seemed to have some hints of pink in it too.

I'd been on the verge of contradicting Rush's statement about me being hot and smart, but the single rose he was holding between his fingers took my breath away. I looked up at him in surprise.

"I didn't know which color you liked, so the guy at the flower shop suggested I pick one based on its meaning. I picked lilac because it represents happiness. That and love at first sight. I guess most of your romance books don't do love at first sight—

I shook my head and sniffed back the tears. "Those were always my favorite," I admitted. "It's beautiful, Rush."

"You're beautiful," Rush responded. He brushed his mouth gently over mine and then handed me the flower. I didn't miss the way his hand trembled just a bit as he held it out for me to take.

I took it and used my free hand to dash at my eyes to try and keep the tears at bay.

"I wasn't sure if you had a vase for it or not, so the guy from the flower shop suggested I get one just in case and I could always return it if you didn't."

Rush reached past me again to grab a beautiful crystal vase that would fit the rose perfectly. He turned around and went to the sink to fill the vase with water.

"Turns out the guy is married to one of your uncles. His name is Aleks. He's married to Vaughn."

When Rush turned around, he came to a stop, probably because I was still standing shell-shocked in the same spot.

"Christopher?" Rush said softly. I opened my mouth to respond, but all that threatened to come out was a harsh sob. Rush quickly came around the island, setting the vase down in the process. He repeated my name, but all I could do was shake my head because the emotions had effectively rendered me mute.

"Christopher, look, I didn't tell him the flower was for you. I mean, I introduced myself since Vaughn and I know each other, but there's no way they'll know that I got that rose… fuck!" Rush bit out as he ran his fingers through his hair in that nervous way of his. "And it doesn't need to mean anything, especially the whole love at first sight stuff because I know you're not ready for that, but I just knew in my heart it was the one—"

I didn't need to even think about what I was doing. I stepped into Rush's space and wrapped my hand around the back of his neck so I could pull him down for a kiss.

A real one.

One that wouldn't leave him with any doubt about what I was feeling.

It took Rush all of three seconds to kiss me back. I could feel his relief in the way he kissed me, held me. Only when the kiss began to cause us both to overheat did Rush tear his mouth from mine. "Fuck, don't scare me like that again," he complained as he appeared to try and catch his breath.

"Sorry," I said softly. "I don't have any vases," I added, hoping that was enough to explain why I'd gotten so upset at the sight of the beautiful flower.

Rush hesitated a moment and then wrapped his arms around me. "You'd better get some," he murmured. The idea that he was going to keep giving me flowers made my heart hurt. Rush was on a playing field I had no hope of reaching. He was romantic, kindhearted, thoughtful, protective, and said what was in his heart.

I mentally pushed the thought away because I didn't want to ruin the moment. I glanced at the rose.

"So is all this—the flower, the breakfast—some kind of apology for trying to burn my house down, or were you planning to do that wall by wall," I asked as I glanced at the wall between the kitchen and the dining room. It now had several larger holes that I was able to see through.

"Your little pinholes were driving me crazy," Rush groused.

"Um, okay, but Rush…" I began carefully.

"Yeah?"

"I changed my mind about that wall. I was going to patch up the holes I'd made and leave the wall like it is… *was*."

Rush's arms tensed, and then he was dropping them and looking in horror at the decimated wall. "Fuck, Christopher, I'm so sorry. I can put it back—"

I let loose the laugh I'd been struggling to contain. Rush went completely silent, and then his jaw hardened. "You're going to pay for that," he said sternly, though only humor danced in his eyes.

"Wait, is that more smoke?" I said as I pointed at the oven. The second Rush looked over his shoulder, I hightailed it out of the kitchen and made a dash for the stairs.

He caught me halfway up. His big arms caged me against the wall. "Just for that, you're making the pancakes," Rush said. We were both breathing heavily, but it had nothing to do with the short chase.

I let out a soft moan when Rush closed his mouth over mine. The searing kiss had me practically curling my toes. But Rush ended it too quickly, causing a little whimper of protest to escape my lips.

"Will you go out with me?" Rush asked suddenly, all humor gone. In its place was what I could only classify as desperate hunger.

Like my answer would determine the fate of the world.

I supposed it would… his and mine anyway.

I knew what I was supposed to say. It would be the easiest and cleanest way to accomplish what needed to be done.

"When?" I asked.

Definitely *not* the word that the voice of doubt had ordered me to say. I had no idea what the hell I was doing. I knew this thing with Rush needed to come to a quick and clean end, but I couldn't let him go.

Not yet.

The worst part was that I was acting out of pure selfishness. While I no longer had any doubt that Rush truly believed he had feelings for me, there would come a day when he wanted out. Even if by some miracle the antiviral therapy finally began to work and my viral load became undetectable, what could I offer a man like Rush? My life was a mess and would be for the foreseeable future. I didn't even have a plan for myself, so how could I hope to build something with a man who deserved so much more. And if I did get sick, Rush would waste days, weeks, months caring for me because he felt obligated to do so.

"Today," Rush said. He leaned down and kissed me softly. "Now."

I nodded without hesitation.

"You aren't working today, right?" Rush asked.

"No."

"Will you show me around Seattle?" Rush asked. "King's tour guide skills are somewhat lacking. I know where the bar that serves the best peanuts is and what to order from the menu at a place where you have to talk into a whale's mouth, but that's pretty much it."

I laughed. That *definitely* sounded like my uncle. He was a man of simple tastes.

"Is there anything in particular you want to see?" I asked. I was already planning out a route that would include many of my favorite places.

"I want to see it all," Rush responded. "But let's start with a place that serves a good breakfast."

"I'll go get ready," I said. "I, um, don't have a car. I use my bike to get where I need to go."

"Bike sounds good," Rush said.

I shook my head because trying to get to all the places by bicycle would be impossible, especially with my hand. I opened my mouth to explain that, but Rush kissed me hard and then wrapped his fingers around my uninjured hand.

"Before I forget…" he said as he led me up to my bedroom.

Butterflies danced in my stomach as I thought about an impromptu make-out session on my bed. But it wasn't the bed he led me to. It was the sizeable walk-in closet. I usually left it open a little so Pip could get in and out to get to the litter box and his food, but the door was completely shut. Rush opened the closet door all the way.

"Okay, guys, noisy stuff is over," he said. A moment later, Pip wobbled his way out of the closet. Right on his heels was a huge, white rabbit with floppy ears. Rush glanced at me and said, "I didn't want the noise to scare Pip, so I brought him some company."

"Oh my God," I said as I watched the kitten and the rabbit interact. The rabbit appeared to be guiding Pip away from things the kitten could stumble over like the little handheld vacuum cleaner I kept just outside the closet and one of the decorative pillows that had fallen to the floor at some point, probably while Rush and I had been watching movies the night before.

"Thumper's a good mama," Rush added as he crouched down. I did the same. Thumper immediately began nudging Pip toward us.

"Awww, thank you, sweetie," I said as I ran my hand over the rabbit's silky soft fur. Pip, meanwhile, had taken the opportunity to sit next to the bunny and use her body as leverage so he could groom himself.

"Thumper is litter box trained, so she won't make a mess, and I got her stuff set up in the closet next to Pip's. But if you don't want—"

"I want," I interrupted. I looked at Rush. "Thank you." I glanced at the rose I was still holding on to as well as the animals. "You've been busy," I said.

"I had a plan to execute and needed the head start," Rush corrected. He gave me a peck on the lips and said, "Go get ready. We need to make a stop at my hotel before breakfast." Rush took the rose from me and helped me stand. "Don't forget your meds," he added. He hesitated and then added, "Sorry, you know what you need to do. I'll stop doing that."

"Doing what?" I asked in confusion.

"Nagging you to remember to take them. You've been dealing with this by yourself for a long time now, and you don't need someone riding you all the time."

"Riding me?" I asked, raising my brows a bit.

"Jesus, fuck, no, not riding you like riding you—"

"You're too easy," I said with a laugh. I wrapped my arms around Rush, who was growling something under his breath that probably had to do with my supposed punishment. But he didn't hesitate to return the embrace. "And you're not nagging," I said against his neck. "I like knowing that someone is watching out for me." Nervous energy flowed through me as I added, "I like knowing that *you're* watching out for me, Rush."

"Always, Christopher. Always."

CHAPTER ELEVEN

RUSH

14

"That's not a bike… that's a… that's a…"

I watched in amusement as Christopher stared at my Harley.

As soon as we'd left his house in my car, he'd reminded me that we needed to grab his bicycle. I'd ignored him, and when he'd questioned what I was doing, I'd simply told him he'd see soon enough. The drive to my hotel had taken only a few minutes, but the ride was so very different from the one when I'd driven him to get his hand stitched up.

Christopher was relaxed and light. I'd never seen him smile so much. And he touched me.

A lot.

Mostly just to get my attention as he pointed out some interesting sight or landmark, but the Christopher from three days ago wouldn't have done that. Nor would he have joked around with me and even pranked me.

I wasn't foolish enough to believe it would be unicorns and rainbows from here on out, but I wanted to believe I'd gotten past enough of Christopher's walls to reach the real him. I was fully expecting him to lash out verbally or shut down completely in the future as our relationship intensified, but I was ready for it.

He was scared.

I got that.

I was terrified but for entirely different reasons. I knew how fragile life could be and how easily it could be snuffed out. Add in the fact that I knew next to nothing about Christopher's prognosis, and I was a mess. I just did a really good job of hiding it.

"You game?" I asked Christopher. We'd already been inside my room so he could meet the other four rabbits I called family. He'd fallen in love with the little critters but hadn't liked my lack of creativity when he'd learned the names of the last three rabbits I'd gotten.

"Thumper, Bugs, Three, Four, and Five," Christopher had chided, his long arms crossed in front of him. "Yeah, that needs to change."

I'd merely smiled and told him to get on it.

Now if I could only get him on the Harley.

"Aren't these things called donor cycles or something like that?" Christopher asked.

I moved to stand next to Christopher. "Helmets," I said as I pointed at the two helmets hanging off the handlebars. "Precious cargo," I continued as I looked him up and down. "And the best damn teacher no amount of money can buy... my dad. Even if he hadn't already been so safety conscious himself, my mother's very creative threats of bodily harm if I ended up with even so much as a scratch made sure I knew the ins and outs of riding a motorcycle long before I even got on it."

"Your dad taught you to ride motorcycles?" Christopher asked.

I nodded. "Ride them, fix them. This was his," I said as I motioned to the bike. A pang of sadness came over me when I added, "We restored it together right after I left the army. The plan was to find another one to restore for me..." I fell silent as I thought about my parents.

Christopher's arm came around me, and then he was leaning his head on my arm. His fingers twined with mine. No words were spoken, but he'd said a million things with the one little gesture.

"Let's do it," he said.

And with that, date number one commenced.

Spending time with Christopher was like watching the sun break through the darkest of storm clouds. As soon as I explained that we'd be able to talk to each other through the helmets' built-in communication systems, he was off and running with the tour. Seeing the city through his eyes was unlike anything I'd expected. Of course, he knew about all the major tourist spots in the area, but his knowledge of the history and culture of each neighborhood that made up the city was amazing, especially considering he'd only spent a few of his last teenage years in Seattle.

We spent most of the morning slowly driving through the city and making a plan for the spots we wanted to check out on foot. When it came time to find some lunch, Christopher had suggested we take the ferry across the sound and check out some of the local cafes.

After a little bit of awkwardness when we were first seated at our table, we just fell into a conversation, which then led to another and another. Occasionally, there would be these little lulls where we just looked at one another.

Like now.

It wasn't uncomfortable or weird. It was... easy. It was talking without talking.

"How was everything?" our waitress asked when she stopped by our table.

"Amazing," Christopher said.

"Unbelievable," I chimed in.

"How about some dessert?"

When we'd sat down, I'd noticed Christopher looking through the dessert menu, so I said, "Sure, that would be great."

"Rush, no, I'm too full," Christopher said.

"We'll eat it slowly," I responded with a grin. To the waitress, I said, "Can we have the lava cake? Two forks. Some more coffee would be great too."

"Absolutely. Did you want ice cream with the cake?"

I looked pointedly at Christopher. He hesitated, then nodded. "Yes, please. Thank you."

Once she was gone, Christopher shook his head at me and said, "You're a bad influence."

"Can't argue with that," I responded. I leaned forward, putting my elbows on the table, mirroring Christopher's stance. It closed the distance between us considerably.

"How did you get your name?" Christopher asked. "Were you named after a character in a book or movie, or is it a family name?"

I laughed. "Hardly. My parents named me Rush because I was in such a rush to be born that my dad had to deliver me on the side of the road in the middle of the night."

Christopher laughed. "I wish I could have met them," he said softly.

"Me too. They would have loved you."

"So you were out to them?"

I nodded. "I was fifteen when I decided to tell them. I'd heard all the horror stories about kids being kicked out after they came out, so I was terrified I'd be on the streets. I even went so far as to pack a suitcase with a few changes of clothes, some protein bars, and all the cash I'd saved."

"What happened?"

"I kept chickening out for like three weeks. One Saturday afternoon when I got home after mowing a neighbor's lawn, I went to my closet so I could put the money in the suitcase. But when I opened it, there was a piece of paper in it with my name on it. It said, 'Is there any chance you can tell us what you need to tell us by next weekend? We want to borrow your suitcase for our cruise.'"

"Oh my God, what?" Christopher said in surprise.

I nodded. "My parents were like that. Straight to the point."

"What did you do?"

"I emptied out the suitcase, took it downstairs to the kitchen where my parents were making dinner, and that was it. I told them I liked boys as much as I did girls. They hugged me, told me they loved me, and then started asking me questions about my love life," I said.

"Wow, that's amazing."

I smiled. "*They* were amazing."

Christopher reached across the table and took my hand in his. "Can I ask how you lost them?"

My gut automatically tightened like it always did when I thought about how my parents had lost their lives. "They were vacationing in the Big Sur area. They'd rented a really nice house where they were planning on hosting some of their friends from their college days. The place had to be worth around five million bucks or something, but apparently the rental company couldn't be bothered to put up a few carbon monoxide detectors. My parents went to sleep that first night and never woke up again."

"Rush," Christopher whispered, then dropped his eyes and shook his head. His fingers were tight around mine.

I pulled his hand to me and dropped a kiss on his fingers. "They went together," I said. "That brings me a lot of comfort."

Christopher nodded. He wiped at his eyes before lifting them again. The waitress chose that moment to return with our dessert.

"Wow," I said because the dish was huge. I handed Christopher a fork and said, "Would you do the honors?"

He smiled and took the fork, then proceeded to cut the cake until the hot chocolate filling began oozing out of it.

"Bon appétit," Christopher said as he held up his fork. I touched my fork to his and then dug in. As delicious as the dessert was, seeing how much pleasure it brought Christopher was a thousand times more satisfying. I couldn't help but wonder when the last time he'd indulged in anything was.

I waited until Christopher had seemingly finished before I took a chance and broached the topic I'd been thinking about ever since Christopher had told me what Peter had done to him.

"Christopher, why didn't you call your uncle and Con when you found out about Peter? Why have you been going through all this alone?"

Christopher's expression tensed as he leaned back in his chair. But to my surprise, he didn't remain silent.

"At first I didn't want to believe it. I couldn't. So I just pretended it wasn't even a thing. I went on with life as usual. It took a whole month for me to get up the nerve to get tested and then another two weeks to make the appointment to get the results. I didn't tell anyone because I knew I was fine. I didn't feel sick, so that meant I had to be fine. But I knew as soon as I sat down in that chair and looked at the lady on the other side of the desk that I wasn't fine."

Christopher paused, seemingly to collect himself. Unlike when he'd talked about his decision to isolate himself from the world after the attack in the club, this time around his voice broke here and there, proof he wasn't disconnecting from his emotions.

"The clinic gave me a ton of information about the next steps, but everything was a blur. I didn't cry, I didn't tell them they'd made a mistake and they needed to test me again… it was like that night at the club… I had no control, no fight in me. As strange as it may sound, that actually helped. As a nurse, you have to learn to keep a certain level of detachment from your patients even as you're giving them the best care you can. So I decided to do that. I detached from it."

Christopher reached for his coffee and took a sip. I could see that his hand was shaking. Since I wasn't sure if he wanted to be touched or not, I simply let my boot slide up against his shoe underneath the table to remind him he wasn't alone now.

"I kept up my normal life of studying while Positive Christopher did what he was told and began seeing doctors and counselors and taking all the pills they gave him. It took a while for me to accept reality and really begin to participate in my treatment. When I started to understand what viral loads were, it became this waiting game. My viral load was around thirty thousand copies when it was first checked."

"Copies?" I asked.

"Yeah, the virus copies itself. It reproduces."

I'd been trying to remain calm, but the more Christopher talked, the more agitated I became.

The virus was fucking reproducing inside of his body? Possibly even right now, even as we spoke?

"Is that high?" I asked.

"Yes and no," Christopher responded. "Basically, the higher number of copies means the disease is progressing more quickly. It can get as high as a million copies."

"Fuck," I whispered.

"Yeah," Christopher responded.

I felt Christopher's foot press harder against mine.

"They started me on a combination of ART drugs. Antiretroviral therapy," Christopher explained. "I was so scared, Rush," he admitted softly.

I reached my hand across the table. I was glad when Christopher leaned in and took it. His hand was cold and clammy, proof that this discussion wasn't easy for him. "I know you were, baby," I said. "How about we take a walk?" I suggested.

Christopher nodded.

I quickly paid the check, left a healthy tip, and led Christopher from the restaurant. I'd spied a small park with a walking path on the way into the small town, so I knew it was close by, and we wouldn't need my bike to get to it. I held Christopher's hand as we walked past some small shops.

"I wanted to call Uncle Micah and Con more than anything," Christopher said. "Even though I was so ashamed of how I'd ended up in the situation, I was more scared of the unknown."

"So why didn't you?"

"I realized that not knowing was the part that was slowly killing me. I couldn't eat or sleep. I couldn't concentrate on anything. Luckily, I'd finished my finals by then, but that also meant no more studying, so I had even more time to think about what could happen. I couldn't put Uncle Micah and Con through that. I couldn't watch them suffer. I couldn't be the cause of their suffering. I knew I'd made the right decision when I got tested again after taking the ART meds for a month. My count had actually gone higher. Not by much, but it just made everything worse. I, um, started to have some pretty dark thoughts," Christopher admitted.

I couldn't contain the rush of air that left my lungs. We'd reached the park, but instead of walking, I led Christopher to a stone bench between two trees. As soon as we sat, I pulled him against me.

We sat there in silence for a long time, but I never loosened my hold on him, and his grip on me never wavered.

"What made you decide to come home?" I asked. "You were just starting your treatment at that time, right?"

Christopher nodded. "When the count went up instead of down, I knew I needed to go home. Even if I couldn't be with my family the way I wanted, knowing they were nearby helped. It reminded me that I had something to live for. But I still wasn't willing to put them through the not knowing what was going to happen. It's something that consumes my thoughts day in and day out. I look at things like these trees, but I can't see their beauty. All I can think about is will I be here next year to see them? It's like that with so many things."

"Christopher…" I whispered, my voice breaking. "Is that's why it's so hard for you to see your family?"

Christopher let out a half sob and nodded. "Every time I see any one of them, I just want to tell them the truth so they can tell me I'll be okay, that I'll be here next year."

I closed my arms around Christopher hard and kissed the top of his head as he sobbed against my chest. "You *will* be here next year, do you hear me? And the year after that and the year after that. You're going to be around to help me to remember to put my dentures in, and you're going to yell all the stuff from the news into my ear because I can't hear the damn thing and am too stubborn to get a hearing aid. Do you hear me?" I asked almost angrily.

Christopher nodded despite the fact that he was still crying. When we'd both managed to calm down, Christopher sat up and used his sleeve to wipe at his eyes. "Do tears on the first date mean there probably won't be a second?" he said with a laugh. He seemed a little lighter. Some of the color was returning to his skin, and his eyes seemed brighter.

"The way I heard it is that whoever cries on the first date is the one who has to propose."

The comment had Christopher laughing. He leaned against my side and put his head on my shoulder.

"Where do things stand now with your count?" I asked. I hated to have to bring the issue up, but I needed to know. Not just so I could support him but so I could join him on that roller coaster that had two potential outcomes.

"It's stayed the same despite changing the medications. Dr. Kleinman added in a couple more drugs. I get tested next week to see what the count is. If it hasn't gone down… I guess… I guess I don't know what will happen then. My life has kind of been on hold, so I haven't enrolled in the BSN program, and I haven't gotten my RN license. Why start something I might not be able to finish?"

We both fell silent. A gamut of emotions was coursing through me. It reminded me of the seven stages of grief. I was certainly dealing with several of them, including bargaining, anger, and denial. I understood why Christopher didn't want to put his family through this, but I also knew they would want to know so they could support him. Not knowing and pretending life was normal or trying to figure out why their loved one had returned home so very different had to be nearly as torturous as dealing with the truth.

It wasn't a decision I could make for him. I could only decide for myself how I'd deal with it, and that didn't even require any thought.

I wasn't going anywhere.

But I was also clueless as to how to help Christopher. It was just one big waiting game.

"Tell me what you need me to do, Christopher," I said as I held his hand and stared at the people across the street who were going on about their lives while the beautiful young man next to me waited to see what his own future would be… or if he even had one. If *we* had one.

Christopher sighed and squeezed my hand.

"You're doing it, Rush. You're doing it."

CHAPTER TWELVE

CHRISTOPHER

44

I was nervous.

No, not nervous.

Terrified.

I'd only been in the nervous stage for the last half an hour of our day of sightseeing. The terrified part had come in shortly after we'd returned the Harley to the hotel parking lot and checked on Rush's bunnies.

The thing that had flipped that switch from nervous to terrified?

Something completely ridiculous, something not even worthy of a second thought, especially considering how our date was supposed to have been a onetime thing.

But leave it to me to allow every ounce of joy I'd felt for so much of the day to fall by the wayside because of one simple thing.

Rush hadn't grabbed any clothes as we'd left.

I was freaking out because the man had several boxes and suitcases full of his personal belongings in his hotel room, and he hadn't grabbed any of it.

He hadn't grabbed any of it because he was planning on *returning* to the room.

Tonight.

After he dropped me off.

"Hey, you okay?" Rush asked as his fingers brushed over mine where they were resting on the console that separated the front seats of the huge pickup truck.

I nodded. "Just tired," I said. It wasn't a lie. I *was* tired. But every ounce of exhaustion had been worth it. My day with Rush had been like a dream. It had been as perfect as the rare weather. Even with the stuff we'd talked about at lunchtime, it hadn't taken long to get back the natural high I'd been riding all morning. A lot of that had to do with the fact that I got to have my arms wrapped around Rush's strong body pretty much all day. I'd like the motorcycle more than I'd thought I would, but knowing I would get to hold on to Rush would be the main reason I'd say yes if he asked me to go for a ride again.

Except *that* was more and more unlikely to happen.

I sighed as we made the turn onto my road. Moments later, we were pulling into the driveway.

"Well, thank you for today," I said awkwardly as I got myself unbuckled. "I had a lot of fun."

God, I didn't even sound like an actual person.

Escape.

Get up and out. Easy peasy.

Except not quite peasy because Rush grabbed my arm before I could open the door. "You sure you're okay?"

I nodded. "Yeah, yeah, I'm great." I gently tugged my arm free and got out of the car. I was certain I'd made a clean break until I heard a car door slam and footsteps behind me. I half turned as I walked and said, "It's okay, you don't need to walk me to the door. I'm sure you have things you need to do."

I didn't give Rush time to respond. I just dashed to the door and began searching my pockets for the keys. I could still hear footsteps behind me, so I knew Rush had ignored my comment. My fingers shook as I tried to put the key in the lock. I let out a little gasp when Rush's big hand closed over mine. He was practically pressed up against my back.

"Why are you trying to run away from me?" Rush asked softly, his breath tickling the back of my neck. Then his lips were skimming over the same spot.

"I'm not. I just—" I didn't know how to finish the sentence because I was clueless as to what was happening. Maybe he just wanted an end of the first date kiss?

"Just what?" Rush asked as he nuzzled my ear. A violent tremor jolted through my body. I barely managed to stifle a moan. I dropped my head forward so he could give the same level of attention to the back of my neck.

I was caught in a haze of desire as my mind and body warred within one another.

Not a good combination.

Unfortunately, my mind won out. "Thumper!" I said as I realized Rush was following me because he needed to collect his pet. I snapped my head up and met something that was both hard and soft at the same time.

"Ow, fuck!" Rush shouted as he took several steps backward, his hands covering his nose.

His very bloody nose.

My own head hurt like hell, but the sight of Rush bleeding had me rushing forward. Unfortunately, Rush unknowingly stepped off the porch step. He tried to catch himself, but in my haste to grab his arm, I too lost my balance and fell forward.

And that was all she wrote.

Our only saving grace was that we landed on the grass next to the walkway leading to the porch. *My* saving grace was that I landed on top of Rush's hard body instead of the harder ground.

Sadly, grace wasn't watching over Rush, who took the brunt of my weight when he hit the ground.

"Oh God, Rush, are you okay?" I asked as I instinctively reached for his face.

"You were soooo close to getting the Tour Guide of the Year award," Rush groused. He let his arms fall flat on the grass. I scooted up his body to examine his nose.

"I'm so sorry," I said as I tried to gently wiggle his nose back and forth.

"Son of a bitch," Rush growled, but he didn't make a move to stop me.

"Well, the good news is it's not broken," I said.

"What's the bad news?" Rush said, his head rolling enough so he could look at me. Despite the injury, he didn't actually seem all that upset. In fact, one of his hands lifted to cradle my hip as I held there on all fours with my face just inches from his.

"The bad news is you didn't break anything of mine, so I'm not going to get another antique out of this."

It took Rush a second to process my words, and then he burst out laughing.

"Ow, shit, that hurts," he moaned as he grabbed his nose.

"Let's get some ice on it," I said. I began to lift off him, but that hand on my hip tightened. I got the silent message and stayed put.

Rush's eyes grew serious. "Why were you running?" he asked. His hand moved from my hip to my face. He brushed some stray hair behind my ear as his eyes pinned mine.

"You didn't take any clothes," I admitted, my cheeks heating.

"What?" Rush said with a shake of his head.

"At the hotel, you didn't grab a change of clothes or a toothbrush or…" I let the words die off as I considered how ridiculous I'd acted.

"So you thought I wasn't going to stay with you tonight," Rush murmured. "So while you were spending the entire ride home upset about me leaving, I was trying to figure out how to convince you to let me spend the night with you again."

"What?" I asked in surprise. "You… you want to stay tonight?"

"For starters," Rush said. Then in one graceful move, he rolled our bodies so I was beneath him on the cool grass. Rush turned his head so he could wipe the majority of the already drying blood on his sleeve. "Did I get enough off?" he asked.

I didn't need to wonder why he wanted to know that. I already knew. I answered him by pulling him down and brushing my lips over his. I was mindful of his injury and kept the kiss soft. He returned the kiss with the same level of sweetness. It wasn't until someone discreetly coughed nearby that we both remembered where we were.

I was horrified to see three older women standing not more than two feet from us. I put them in their late thirties, early forties. One of them was holding what looked like some kind of wicker basket, another had a covered cake pan, and the third was carrying a bottle of wine.

"Oh, God," I said as I tried to push Rush off me.

"Ladies," Rush said in amusement as he made a big production of climbing to his feet and then pulling me up against him.

There was no missing the women's responses as they eyed Rush up and down. I was the one who had to cough to get their attention so they'd stop ogling my guy.

My guy? What the hell?

"Oh, um, good evening," the woman in the middle said. "We're the official welcoming committee," she added. "I'm Margie, and this is Amanda, and that's Theresa." She pointed at the other two women as she introduced them. "Is one of you the homeowner?"

"Um, yeah, that's me," I said. I felt like my cheeks were on fire. So much for living unnoticed in the neighborhood. I'd be lucky if there weren't religious zealots pounding on my door within the hour to tell me I was going to hell.

"This is Christopher," Rush said. "And I'm his boyfriend, Rush."

I nearly swallowed my tongue when he said boyfriend.

"Oh," Margie responded, though admittedly it sounded like she was more interested than disgusted. I didn't see any kind of judgment in the expressions of the other two women either.

"Oh my, are you all right?" Theresa asked Rush as she motioned to his nose.

"Oh yeah, this one doesn't know his own strength," he said as he gave me a little half hug. "He thought he saw a mosquito on my face, and well…" Rush tipped his head and motioned to his nose.

"No, I—"

"Is that a merlot?" Rush asked Amanda, who was holding the bottle of wine.

"Why, yes, it is. It's one of my husband's and my favorite vintages. We hope you enjoy it."

"And this is just a little basket of goodies from some of the different small businesses in the area," Margie added. "But the real treat is Theresa's homemade Lemon Surprise cake."

Theresa lifted the cake cover off to reveal a gorgeous layer cake with white frosting and yellow shavings along with a few lemon slices.

"Wow," Rush and I said in unison.

"Anyway, we don't want to keep you," Margie said with a sly smile as she handed me the basket and the wine. Rush was given the cake.

"If you drop that," I warned him.

"Not a chance," Rush responded. He was practically salivating.

"Thank you so much," I said. "I, uh, wow, this is just really nice."

"It's no trouble," Amanda said, and then she was giving me a hug despite the stuff in my arms. As the ladies said their goodbyes, a strange sense of loss came over me. I glanced at Rush, but he didn't say anything, though I had a feeling he knew what I was going through.

"Um, would you ladies like to come inside? There's way too much here for just me and Rush," I said. As right as the invitation felt, I was also a little terrified by it. I'd been living a low profile for so long that I wasn't sure I even knew how to entertain guests.

The ladies turned their heels on a dime.

"We couldn't…"

"Just for a little while…"

"Wine and a Theresa cake? Jay is going to be so jealous," Margie said.

"Oh, well, you can invite him if you want," I offered.

"He's a she, and she's out of town," Margie said easily. "Married for fifteen years, and I still can't sleep without her next to me. I'm sure you know what I'm talking about." Margie put her arm around me as she grabbed the bottle of wine and cast a glance at Rush, who was surrounded by the other two women.

I should have used the opportunity to correct what Rush had said about being my boyfriend, but the words wouldn't come. Instead, I responded to her comment about not being able to sleep without my man by my side with total honesty.

"I do," I agreed. I looked over my shoulder at Rush, who shot me a wink even as he charmed the ladies.

He hadn't even been sharing my bed for more than a couple of days, but I couldn't even fathom what it would be like to one day have to sleep without him by my side.

It was insanity.

As Margie urged me toward the house, I realized something.

Maybe a little insanity was just what the doctor ordered.

CHAPTER THIRTEEN

RUSH

†4

The next several days flew by in most ways but dragged in one very important one.

Christopher had had his blood drawn the previous day so the RNA test to check his viral count could be run. The results would take anywhere from two to four days to get. Although we tried to stay busy, there was no denying that both of us were needing *and* dreading the call that the results were in. Even then, there would be more waiting because the doctor would only share the results with Christopher in person, not over the phone. Based on her schedule, it could take another day or two to get in to see her.

So keeping busy was vital.

During the day, I worked on some of the remodeling projects Christopher had mentioned while he worked in his room, where he had a small nook that was just big enough for a desk. At night we held each other as we watched movies and talked about everything and nothing. I'd learned more about Christopher's childhood both before and after Con had come into their lives. It had been the death of Christopher's father that had brought the MMA fighter into Micah's life, and while it had been a bumpy journey, there was no doubt that

Christopher considered Micah and Con his fathers even if he didn't call them that.

In turn, I'd told him about how I'd planned to live in Colorado close to my folks. Since my work required a lot of travel, I'd been living out of hotels pretty much nonstop, but I'd been ready to set up a home base somewhere, and that somewhere was supposed to have been Colorado.

They were all the conversations that normal people had long before they began playing house, but our way worked for us. After the bloody nose thing, there'd been no more talk of whether or not I was staying over. In fact, Christopher had taken it a step further by insisting we gather up the rest of my four-legged brood and bring them back to the house with us. The bunnies spent most of the day eating through all the overgrown grass and vegetation in the less than tidy fenced-in backyard.

Except Thumper.

She was too busy sticking to Pip's side like glue. The pair had become inseparable, and they were so damn cute together, Christopher and I often joked that they needed their own social media page.

As smoothly as things were going, there was one glaring sticking point that neither of us talked about.

His family.

Specifically, King.

I still had a job to do, and that kept me in daily communication with King. I often went to his and Gio's house to work with King on logistics and strategy, but I hadn't once mentioned my relationship with Christopher. Even on the multiple occasions that the topic of Christopher had come up between Gio and King while I'd been there and I'd been forced to see how devastated Gio was by the turn his and Christopher's relationship had taken, I'd stayed silent. When Gio and King had told me they'd put their wedding on hold because Gio wanted Christopher to be his best man but wasn't sure his onetime best friend would say yes, I'd actually had to make up an excuse to leave because I'd been so fucking torn up inside for all of them.

My hope was that the next round of Christopher's testing would be the catalyst that brought him back to his family. Even if the news wasn't good, it was more apparent than ever that Christopher needed to come home.

For real this time.

"Oh, wow," I heard Christopher say from behind me as he stepped out onto the back porch. "Rush, it's gorgeous!"

I loved how he immediately came to me and put his arm around me.

"I still need to stain it, but I'll need you to pick out what color you want. I can also just paint it if you prefer—"

Christopher's mouth on mine shut me up. Unfortunately, it was over too soon. "What I want is to try it out," Christopher said, and then he was closing his fingers around mine. He sat gingerly on the gliding bench and smiled when it rocked back and forth just a tiny bit as he sat. I sat down next to him and automatically put my arm around his shoulder.

"It's perfect," Christopher whispered.

I'd built the gliding bench after Christopher had mentioned wanting to put some kind of seating on the back porch so we could watch the rabbits frolic or just enjoy the weather. It had taken me four days of nearly nonstop work, but I'd pulled it off, and I'd even managed to surprise Christopher with it. He'd assumed I'd been working on some shelving in the garage. While Christopher's tool kit had been a little on the sparse side (three screwdrivers and a hammer), thankfully, I'd had all of my father's tools in storage, so it had just been a matter of getting everything set up in the garage.

As I leaned back against the bench, I used my boot to get it moving. Christopher's hand came up to cover the one I had on his shoulder. I could feel the stitches against my own skin.

"How's this feeling?" I asked as I turned my hand a bit so we could twine our fingers together.

"Good," Christopher said with a nod. "Dr. Kleinman said she'll take the stitches out when I go in for the results."

"When *we* go in," I corrected.

"Rush—"

"We're not having this conversation again," I interrupted. "I'm coming with you, and that's that. I know you can keep me from coming in the room with you, but I'll be parked in the waiting room, and the second we're in my truck, you *will* tell me everything." I lightened my statement by adding, "You don't want to test my powers of persuasion, Christopher."

Christopher chuckled and dropped his head to my shoulder.

"I heard you talking to Uncle King this morning," Christopher said softly. "I wasn't eavesdropping or anything, I was just coming downstairs to get something to drink—"

"It's okay, I heard you on the stairs. I was going to tell you about it tonight over dinner. No secrets, right?"

Christopher nodded. "You turned down a job, didn't you? For me. You told Uncle King you had to go to Colorado to deal with some estate stuff."

I sighed. "Yes, I turned down a job, but King has plenty of men and women on his team who can handle that kind of job. Since he's joined forces with that Ronan guy's team, our resources are pretty much limitless now. I think he was offering it to me because he probably thought I miss being in the field."

"Do you?" Christopher asked.

I gave the question some thought and was surprised by the answer. "No, I don't actually."

It was the absolute truth. In the past, I couldn't wait to get the call from King that there was a job, but I hadn't missed the boots on the ground stuff at all in the week I'd spent with Christopher.

"I didn't want this," Christopher murmured, pulling me from my thoughts.

"What?" I asked.

"For you to lie to him, to anyone, to protect me."

"You come first, Christopher. Always. I know we've kind of put a pin in it when comes to our relationship and me telling you how I feel about you, but no matter what happens, you will always come first. Do you hear me?"

Christopher nodded and then pressed his entire body against mine. I automatically enfolded him in my arms.

"Rush?"

"Yeah?"

"How do I take it out?"

I stilled. I knew in my gut what he was talking about, but I had to be sure he did too. "Take what out, sweetheart?"

Christopher sat up. He shifted so he was sitting sideways on the bench. I did the same so we could face one another.

"I don't want my life to be on hold anymore. No matter what the results are, I want to live my life. I want to live it with you, Rush, but I know it's a lot to ask—"

I didn't let him finish. I snaked my hand around the back of his neck and slashed my mouth over his. Christopher squeaked in surprise, but then he was eagerly kissing me back. His tongue swept into my mouth, seeking control. I gave it to him. Although we hadn't done more than kiss since that first morning when he'd given me the privilege of being the first one to taste the lush beauty of his mouth, he kissed me like he'd been doing it forever. There was no hesitation, no fear, no confusion. It was just Christopher. The real Christopher.

My Christopher.

I wasn't sure if I pulled Christopher onto my lap or if he ended up there on his own, but I didn't waste the opportunity. I clasped his face and held him as I took ownership of the kiss. As we feasted upon one another, Christopher began grinding his dick against mine. I ached to get my hands on his flesh. I wanted to feel his skin against mine. I wanted to feel his weight on top of me as much as I wanted to sink my weight down on him.

By the time we were forced to come up for air, we were both panting and practically humping each other right there on the pretty new glider.

"Inside," I growled.

I didn't give Christopher a chance to stand. Instead, I grabbed his slim thighs and lifted him as I stood. "Rush, we can't—"

"I know, sweetheart. But there are hundreds of ways for us to make love safely." I pressed a gentle kiss to his mouth. "Pin's out, baby. And it's not going back in for anything. I love you so fucking much, Christopher."

I kissed him before he could respond, but there was no denying how my words had affected him. His mouth was needy and demanding against mine as I tried to maneuver us into the house without putting him down. I somehow managed to get us inside, but when Christopher slid his hand beneath the waistband of my jeans and brushed his fingers over the head of my cock, I knew there was no way I was going to be able to get us to his bed. I'd blow inside my jeans long before that.

The first flat surface I found was the dining room table. As I laid Christopher down on it, his legs remained wrapped around my waist. His slim fingers tugged at my T-shirt, so I reached behind me to pull it over my head and cast it aside. Before I could even cover his body again, he was running his hands over my abdomen. He pulled himself upright and pressed a soft kiss to my sternum.

"I've wanted this for so long," he murmured. His eyes lifted to meet mine. "Do you remember asking me how I knew you'd left the army?"

"Yeah," I said, my breath catching because Christopher's hands were on the move.

South.

"After that night at the club, King talked about you to my Uncle Micah and Con. I was listening from the stairs where they couldn't see me. Anytime anyone talked about you, usually Uncle King, I eavesdropped whenever I could. Then I started having dreams about you. Lots of dreams."

Christopher palmed my dick hard through my pants.

"Fuck," I moaned, and then I was grabbing his face and kissing him hard. I released his mouth long enough to say, "As soon as I saw you, I knew you were meant to be mine."

Christopher let out a little whimper, and then his mouth was back on mine. I pressed him back down on the table and pushed his shirt up, exposing his abdomen. Christopher let out a loud moan as I licked a path down his treasure trail and then mouthed his dick through his sweats.

"Christopher?"

What I'd heard didn't register at first.

"What the fuck? Get the fuck off of him!"

That *did* register. There was someone in the house. I straightened and turned at the same time, putting my body between the assailant and Christopher. I managed to dodge a punch meant for my jaw, but I couldn't do much about being body slammed to the floor. I'd already figured out who the heavy weight on top of me was, but that didn't stop me from throwing my own punch.

King's weight fell off me as my fist caught him underneath the chin.

"Stop it!"

"King, stop!"

The first voice was most definitely Christopher's; the second was Gio's.

I staggered to my feet, but King was faster. He grabbed me by the throat and slammed me against the wall.

"What the fuck are you doing?" he snarled. "He's practically my kid!"

"Get the fuck off me," I snapped as I broke the hold King had on my throat.

"Enough!" Gio yelled, and then he was stepping in front of his fiancé. It did nothing to dim King's rage, but it did keep him from coming after me again.

"We're done!" King declared as he pointed his finger at me. "Lying to me is one thing, but taking advantage of—"

"Stop it!" Christopher screamed at the top of his lungs. It was enough to shut King up. I shoved past him and went to Christopher, who was standing next to the table, his slim arms wrapped around his body.

He was stiff as a board and shaking violently. "Get me a blanket," I ordered King. "It's on the back of the couch."

To my surprise, the man did as I said. I wrapped the throw around

Christopher and turned him to face me. I bent enough so I could look him in the eye. "You're first, Christopher. Always. Remember?"

Christopher hesitated, then nodded his head. He pulled in a deep breath. I was satisfied to see some of the tension leave his body.

"I can make them go," I said softly, though not soft enough so that King wouldn't hear me. I didn't give a shit what the man thought was happening, I wouldn't allow him to put any more strain on Christopher.

Christopher looked at King, then Gio, who was standing only a foot or two from his fiancé. He looked completely shell-shocked.

Something happened in that moment when the two young men's gazes met, because a mere heartbeat later, Christopher let out a harsh sob and walked straight to Gio, who instantly enveloped his best friend in his arms. Tears streaked down Gio's face as Christopher let out a choked "Sorry" before he was consumed by sobs again.

I took the opportunity to grab my shirt and pull it back on. King had calmed down considerably. When he shot me a glance filled with confusion and pain, I let go of my anger and simply stayed off to the side.

After a minute or two, Christopher pulled free of Gio. They smiled shakily at each other before Christopher turned his attention to King.

"Rush lied to you for me," he began. I knew what was coming and wished there was something, anything I could do to make it hurt a little less for everyone in the room.

"He didn't want to leave town because he wanted to be here when I… when I, um…" Christopher paused and glanced over his shoulder at me. I sent him a soft smile and told him with my eyes what I couldn't with my mouth. As much as I loved him, I couldn't do this *for* him. And he still had the opportunity to change his mind. I would happily support any lie he might tell his uncle and best friend because it was about what Christopher needed and no one else.

Christopher took a deep breath. "He wanted to be here when I got some test results back."

I could see the confusion swirling in both men's eyes as they looked between them and Christopher and then even to me. It was heart-wrenching to see the moment when both realized what was happening.

"Christopher?" Gio whispered.

Christopher dropped his eyes briefly, but when he lifted them again, I was so fucking proud of him. His eyes latched onto King's.

"I'm sick, Uncle King."

CHAPTER FOURTEEN

CHRISTOPHER

14

The moment my uncle put his arms around me without saying a word, I knew everything would be okay. Sure, I'd get barraged with questions by him and other family members as I told them, but *this*—this moment of quiet as someone shared their strength would ultimately be what saw me through.

I couldn't say how long King held me for, but when he reluctantly released me and put some space between us, I asked, "I know you both have a lot of questions, but can you ask Uncle Micah and Con to come over first?"

"I'll take care of it," King said without hesitation. I turned and went to Rush, who wrapped his arms around me.

"I'm so fucking proud of you, Christopher," he murmured.

I wanted to tell him I loved him, but I didn't want the first time he heard the words to be under such chaotic circumstances. I'd been on the verge of admitting it to him while he'd had me pressed down on the table I'd never see the same way again, but we'd been interrupted.

"I need to talk to Gio," I said. "Can you two not kill each other while we're gone?" I asked as I looked between Rush and King, speaking loudly enough so my uncle could hear me.

"I can't kill him if I can't see him, and since my retinas burned up at the sight of my nephew being mauled on a table..."

I rolled my eyes and pressed a quick kiss to Rush's mouth before heading for Gio. As I passed my uncle, I said, "Maybe now you'll knock on doors like a normal person instead of picking the lock."

King did the Boy Scout salute but winked at me in the same beat, so I knew the man had no intention of changing his notorious ways. I shook my head at him. But damn if it didn't feel good to just settle back into old roles. I could only hope Micah and Con would be as forgiving.

Once I reached Gio, I wrapped my hand around his. He followed me without hesitation up to my bedroom. Once we were upstairs, I released his hand, but as soon as we looked at each other, we were hugging again.

"I'm so sorry—"

"Christopher—"

We both laughed, and then I led Gio to the bed. We sat on the edge of the mattress but turned so we were basically facing each other. I wasn't surprised when Pip reached a tiny paw out from under the bed and took a swipe at my pant leg. I reached down and wiggled my fingers so he'd come out, then picked him up and deposited him on Gio's lap. Thumper appeared from under the bed almost immediately, so I picked her up and held her in my lap.

"A rabbit?" Gio said in surprise. "Does your family not like traditional pets?" he asked.

I laughed because he was right. My sister, Rory, was the one who'd decided our menagerie should be mostly comprised of things that slithered or hissed or had more than four legs. It had started with Stella, the bearded dragon King himself had given to her years earlier.

"I can't take credit for Thumper," I said. "She belongs to Rush. Along with the other four rabbits that are currently mowing the backyard." I nodded at Pip. "That's Pip. He's mine, but I haven't had him long."

We both fell silent for a moment as we stroked the furry bodies in our respective laps.

"Gio, I owe you an apology. A lot of them, actually," I began.

Gio immediately shook his head and dashed at his eyes. He was older than me by only a couple of years but had one of the softest, kindest hearts of anyone I knew. "No you don't. I wish I could take it back, Christopher. That night. The club. I just wish I could take it back. We shouldn't have been there. You tried to tell me that—"

"No, I didn't," I interrupted. "I wanted to say something, but I couldn't."

"You were being a good friend," Gio murmured.

"Actually, no, I wasn't. A good friend wouldn't have let you go into that place. A good friend would have helped you deal with your anger and hurt so you wouldn't do anything rash. I didn't say anything because I couldn't. Not wouldn't... *couldn't.*"

I paused and then dropped my eyes. "In my house, you didn't make a sound. You didn't do anything to get noticed. But Uncle Micah was never silent. He couldn't be because he needed to protect me and Rory. I always thought of myself as a coward, but I think it had more to do with guilt. I never spoke up for the man who raised me. I never *stood up* for him. I allowed myself to hide in stories where I could be something different. Whether I was Pip in *Great Expectations* learning important lessons," I said as I motioned to the kitten in Gio's lap, "or I was waiting for my hero to come rescue me in some sweeping love story, I chose fantasy over reality because it was easier. I blocked out the things that didn't fit into my happily ever after story."

"But something changed after that night," Gio suggested.

"I'd gotten lucky twice. Uncle Micah saved me the first time, and Rush was there the second time. I had to stop believing in fairy tales because there wasn't always going to be a hero waiting on the other side of the door to save me."

Gio shook his head. "It was my fault, Christopher. I know you want to try and take some of the blame off me, but the only reason you needed rescuing that night is because I fucked up."

"Don't you see though, Gio, it would have happened no matter what. If anything, I was lucky because there *was* someone on the other side of that door. I got the wake-up call I needed, but I escaped the worst of the consequences. So if you need to take all the blame for that night, then do it, but my actions and behavior afterwards were all my own. Shutting you out, shutting our family out, that's on me and me alone."

"Christopher…" Gio whispered.

I knew he wanted to say more, to keep apologizing somehow, so I set Thumper on the bed and then scooted forward enough so I could wrap my arms around Gio. "I forgive you, Gio. Please, please forgive yourself. I want *my* Gio back."

Gio cried softly in my arms for a couple of minutes. When we broke apart, we were each dashing at our own eyes and each other's.

"My Christopher," Gio said with a smile.

The acknowledgement that I was back, the real me, was as overwhelming as it was a relief.

Gio wrapped his hands around mine. He looked down at Pip, who'd drifted off to sleep. "It's bad, isn't it?" he whispered.

I knew what he was talking about, of course, but I didn't know how to answer him. I squeezed his fingers as I considered my words. "I stopped living my life long before I got sick," I said. "Then I met this amazing, kind, strong, sweet, gorgeous, sometimes awkward but always honest man who wants to live his life with me. Not tomorrow, not in five years, not if one thing or another happens. Today. He wants to live his life with me today. He loves me today, now. So no, I don't see anything as bad. If I get to live my life with him for an hour or a day or a year or fifty, nothing is going to stop me from loving every second of it. Nothing."

Gio smiled and squeezed my hands hard. "So you're getting your happily ever after after all," he observed.

I laughed because it was true. Rush had said every love story was different. Different but no less magical.

"He was right," I found myself saying aloud.

"Who? Right about what?"

I shook my head. "Rush and his take on love stories. He was right."

Gio shook my hands enough to pull me from my reverie. "Listen to me," he said sharply, though his eyes were bright with amusement.

"No matter how many amazing orgasms that man gives you or how many perfect, sweet, amazing things he says or does, never, *ever* say those three little words to him. Ever! You will regret it, trust me."

"I can't not tell him I love him, Gio."

"What? No, tell him that all you like. Just don't tell him he's right."

I laughed.

"Oh man, you're going to tell him, aren't you? Okay, you'll need a backup plan. Give me your phone."

I handed my phone over without question. I peeked over the top of the phone to see what Gio was looking up and gasped when I saw a very familiar item.

A pair of hot pink underwear.

The same kind I'd told Gio to buy early on in his back-and-forth relationship with King.

"You've got to be kidding me," I said.

Gio shook his head. "When he starts reminding you he was right about one thing so he must be right about everything, just give him a little peek of these. Buy one in every color—it's more convenient that way." Gio's fingers clicked like wildfire over the keyboard, and before I knew it, the shopping cart was full.

"Um, Gio, hang on a second," I said as I saw his finger hover over the instant-buy option. But my words came too late. It was over and done with before I could stop him.

I dropped my head against the phone that was still in his hands.

"What?" Gio said. "I'm pretty sure I got the right size—"

"It's not that," I cut in as I ran my fingers through my hair.

"Then what? What's wrong?"

"That was Rush's account. You just ordered him a dozen neon-colored man panties," I said with a groan.

"Oh crap," Gio whispered.

Before I could say anything else, a voice yelled out from the bottom of the stairs.

"Sweet pea?" Rush called.

"Um, yes… Bunny?" I responded after my eyes fell on Thumper. Gio began laughing and had to slap a hand over his mouth.

"Please tell me you selected the overnight shipping option for the items you… I… you… ordered for me… you… Me." Rush's stumbling words had me guessing King was close by.

Gio and I took one look at each other and dissolved into a fit of laughter. "Show King the order," Gio called. "He might remember how long it took for that package to come. Honey, I'm talking about the package that—"

I heard Rush cough loudly.

And for a long time.

"It's all good. I'll figure it out!" Rush shouted.

I could faintly hear my uncle say, "What package? What did you order?"

The rest of his words were drowned out by Gio's and my laughter.

God, it was good to be home.

EPILOGUE

RUSH

☦4

ONE YEAR LATER

Margie had been right.

It was hell trying to sleep when your other half wasn't in bed beside you. Thankfully, I only had one more night of it, and then Christopher was all mine again until the next semester when he'd have to be on-site at Duke as part of his nurse practitioner program. After that, he'd graduate, and with any luck, the amount of time we'd have to spend apart after that would be limited to a few days here and there when I might need to travel for my own job.

It had been a busy year since Christopher had told his family the truth. Watching the love of my life break the news of his HIV status had nearly torn me apart. But my suffering had been a drop in the hat compared to what Micah, Con, King, and Gio had had to go through the night King and Gio had discovered Christopher and me going at it on the dining room table. I would never forget the sight of Con and Micah arriving at the house shortly after Gio and Christopher had come down from our bedroom. The couple had been too elated to see Christopher, to get to hold him, to even consider why they'd been invited to the house in the middle of the afternoon in the first place. Thankfully, they hadn't brought Christopher's sister, Rory, with them, since she'd been at a playdate.

It was only when Con and Micah had seen King and Gio sitting in the living room, their hands intertwined and their expressions grim, that they'd realized something was up. Since both men had already known who I was from when I'd taken Christopher home after the night at the club, introductions hadn't really been necessary.

As soon as Micah, the man who'd basically become Christopher's father, had heard the news, he'd been on his feet and pulling Christopher into his arms. Micah's unwavering strength despite his obvious fear and confusion had made it impossible for Christopher to keep his composure, especially once Micah had assured the young man that everything would be okay.

There had been a lot of tears, a lot of questions, and a hell of a lot of rage when the four men had learned how Christopher had been exposed. It was at that point that I'd been forced to step in to make sure the focus remained on Christopher and getting him through the following days as we waited to hear if the treatment was working.

We'd gotten the call less than twenty minutes after Christopher and I had urged everyone to go home several hours later. The small group had agreed that there was no need to tell any additional remaining family members until we knew what Christopher's status was.

While we'd been fortunate enough to get an appointment with Dr. Kleinman the very next morning, it had been a sleepless night for both of us and likely the other two couples as well. It was that same night that Christopher had told me he loved me for the first time. We'd spent the rest of the evening talking about our plans for the future. The issue of Christopher's health hadn't even been a part of the discussion because our future together would be the same whether it lasted days, weeks, months, or years. The reality was that no one, not a single person on the planet, was guaranteed a tomorrow. It was something most took for granted, but not us.

When the time for the appointment had rolled around, Christopher had asked his family to wait at a café near his doctor's office with the excuse that not everyone would fit into Dr. Kleinman's exam room. That part had been true, though the kindly doctor probably could have figured something out. The truth was that Christopher had wanted the two of us to have a few minutes to process the results and what it would mean. When Dr. Kleinman had come into the room and smiled at Christopher, ensuring she had good news, he'd let out this half sob before covering his face with his hands. Although I'd been seated next to him, I'd immediately moved so I could wrap my arms around him, and once he'd composed himself, I'd moved my chair closer to his so there was virtually no space between us.

While his numbers hadn't miraculously dropped to the point that his viral count was undetectable, the fact was that they *had* dropped. Enough so that Dr. Kleinman kept Christopher on the same regimen. A month later, the numbers had gone down again, then again. While Christopher wouldn't allow himself to get his hopes up in the beginning, as each month had gone by and the number had continued to decrease, there was no denying that he'd begun to feel safe enough to hope.

Within six months, Christopher had taken the RN exam and enrolled in the nurse practitioner program at Duke. I'd moved in long before that, and life had become relatively normal and even somewhat anticlimactic. Christopher quit his insurance job and began working part-time for Dr. Kleinman with the intent of staying on staff after he became a nurse practitioner. He spent the rest of the time evenly split between studying and spending time with his family, all of whom knew about his diagnosis by then.

Whenever possible, Christopher and I spent our evenings together, usually exploring some aspect of making love that Christopher was certain wouldn't put me in any kind of danger. Despite having been on PrEP, a drug that prevented HIV, from nearly the beginning of my relationship with Christopher, we hadn't had actual sex until the day he'd gotten the all clear from Dr. Kleinman that his viral load had become undetectable.

When we weren't exploring each other's bodies, we were working our way through his most favorite romance novels, reading sections to each other. Not surprisingly, the hotter parts of the stories were always a considerable distraction, though not an unwelcome one. Once our bodies were sated, it wasn't unusual for one rabbit after another along with a slowly but steadily growing Pip to end up in bed with us, thanks to the little set of steps I'd built the critters that allowed them to get up on and down from the bed with ease.

In between the normal stuff, we focused on remodeling the house, hosting and joining in on neighborhood parties that usually included one of Theresa's famous cakes, or just sitting on our bench over-looking the backyard.

I was doing exactly that as I tried not to think about how many hours I still had before I'd get to video chat with Christopher.

While I'd built the bunnies a sizeable bunny mansion in the back-yard and even given in to Christopher's insistence that we put up some birdproof netting to cover the entire yard so none of our "kids" would be grabbed by a hawk, more often than not, the bunnies were in the house with us when they weren't gorging themselves on grass.

When Christopher had first decided he'd bring in the rabbits each night for dinner, I'd watched on in humor as he'd tried to wrangle them all. Within two days, he'd only had to call out to them, and they were all racing up the steps to wait by the back door.

I sighed because it was yet another moment that made me keenly aware of how much I missed my man.

"Okay, guys," I called as I swallowed down the last of my beer and resigned myself to spending the evening channel surfing surrounded by at least one bunny butt pressed up against some part of my face. "Thumper, Bugs, Hazel, Snowball, Bunnicula, come on, dinnertime."

I couldn't help but smile at the three names Christopher had come up with to replace my ill-advised numbering system. He'd absolutely refused to use Google to find some famous bunny names, but after he'd only managed to come up with Hazel, the only female rabbit name he could remember from *Watership Down*, he'd sought out expert help from a younger generation.

His sister, Rory, had come up with Snowball from the *Pets* movies while Luca's daughter, Violet, had insisted that the last rabbit be named Bunnicula. When questioned, the little girl had insisted not only was Bunnicula a female name but that it fit perfectly because Bunnicula the movie rabbit and our Bunnicula both loved to suck the juice out of vegetables.

Since there was no arguing with that kind of logic, rabbit number five had been christened as such.

As predicted, all the rabbits came hopping up the steps followed by an excited but still pretty wobbly Pip. I was in the process of following everyone inside when something white caught my eye. I looked over my shoulder and saw a white rabbit in the grass. "Snowball, what the hell—" I began only to notice that while the rabbit in the grass was white, it wasn't solid white like Snowball.

I put my beer bottle down and slowly made my way down the porch steps. "Hey, sweetie, where did you come from?" I said softly. Since I'd checked the fence for holes just that morning, there was no way the rabbit had gotten into the yard that way.

To my surprise, the rabbit didn't run away as I approached it. It continued to munch on the grass like I wasn't even there. I gently picked the bunny up but stopped short when I realized the little crea-ture had some kind of sheer, pink material tied around its neck. "What the—" I began but stopped short when a ray of sunlight hit something shiny that was dangling from the makeshift collar. More confused than ever, I lifted the rabbit up higher so I could see what had caught the light. Assuming it was some kind of ID tag, I tried to get a better look, but the bunny wasn't loving the idea of being held so high off the ground, so I tucked her against my chest and searched out the object with my fingers.

As soon as the smooth material hit my skin, I knew what it was.

The soft click of a door shutting had me looking up. I nearly dropped the rabbit in surprise when I saw who it was that was standing on the back porch surrounded by five confused and hungry bunnies and one very happy orange tabby.

"You said you were coming home tomorrow," I blurted even as I drank in the sight of Christopher.

"Did I?" Christopher said in all innocence.

Bullshit innocence.

Not that I cared at all. As he slowly made his way down the stairs, I met him there in just a few big strides. I kissed him before he could object, but when the bunny in my arms began struggling, I realized I'd been squishing the poor thing between us in my haste to get closer to Christopher.

"Hi," I said softly.

"Hi," he said, his skin flush with color. He'd never looked healthier. He'd filled out quite a bit as the stress of his illness waned and his body had started to become used to the medications. But today, there seemed to be just a little bit more pink to his cheeks.

I held up the rabbit a bit. "If you're home early to break up with me, it's not happening," I growled, even though I knew that he had no such plan. Not after feeling what I had on the rabbit's makeshift collar.

"I think the last boyfriend you're ever going to have should be the one to give you your last rabbit," Christopher said with a smile.

"So you're saying no to any more rabbits?" I asked.

Christopher's face fell. "What? No!" he responded. "Just no more breakup bunnies," he clarified.

I nodded and then carefully pulled the bunny's collar over its head before putting the animal back on the ground. All the other rabbits had followed Christopher down the stairs so we were surrounded by the brood. But I had eyes only for Christopher as I searched out the gold band from the folds of the fabric. My heart lurched in my chest as my eyes accepted what my fingers had already felt.

"Did our new girl come with her own bling?" I asked.

Christopher took the ring from my hand and shyly smiled. "You did say whoever cried on the first date had to be the one to propose, right?"

"Yes," I said simply.

"Well, that's good because—"

"Christopher—" I cut in. He stopped toying nervously with the ring and looked up at me. "Yes," I repeated.

It took him a moment to get what I was saying. When he did, a broad smile split his face, and then he launched himself into my arms. I kissed him hard. When we separated, Christopher let out a rough breath. "And to think I was all ready to use these to get my way," he said as he pushed the waistband of his pants down enough to expose the edge of his underwear.

His very pink, very sheer, very snug underwear. He took off for the house before I could pull my tongue back up into my mouth, dancing over the various rabbits as he went. I caught up to him just as he reached the door. I took my time claiming the prize of his mouth. When I had no choice but to catch my breath, Christopher breathed, "I love you, Rush. So much."

"I love you too, my beautiful Christopher."

I pulled him back enough so I could open the door, then started to lead him into the house.

"What about the rabbits?" Christopher asked.

"They'll understand," I responded as I dragged Christopher up against me once we were inside. "They're rabbits, after all."

I kissed him again but kept it chaste.

"Maybe we should make sure they all get along," Christopher said worriedly as he looked in the direction of the backyard.

"Trust me, they're probably explaining to the new girl that you're the easy one."

"Says the man who built them a three-story condo that's bigger than the storage shed."

"You realize you're going to need to come up with another female bunny name, right?" I reminded him.

"I've already got Rory and Violet on it. We should have something by bedtime."

I nodded and glanced out the back door just to make sure the new rabbit truly was being welcomed into the fold. It took me a moment to find her. The black spots were the only thing that distinguished her from Snowball, and they weren't huge spots. When I finally found her, I shook my head.

"Baby, you did make sure this one is a female, right? Or at least a neutered male?" I asked as I watched the new rabbit finish humping Snowball only to start on Hazel next. Christopher's silence spoke volumes.

"Christopher?" I repeated as I pulled my eyes from the debauchery happening in the backyard to my soon-to-be husband.

"Um, what?" Christopher hedged as he began sidling away from me. I opened my mouth to tell him to stay put because I would likely need his help ending the bunny orgy, but then he flashed me another shot of his underwear… this time from behind.

"You're finding all the babies homes," I declared right before I slammed the door to the backyard shut and hightailed it after my man. I followed his laughter all the way up the stairs.

Damn, it was good to have him home.

The End

ABOUT THE AUTHOR

Dear Reader,

I hope you enjoyed Christopher and Rush's story.

Have a pressing question or just a comment you want to share?
Feel free to email me at sloane@sloanekennedy.com

Join my Facebook Fan Group: Sloane's Secret Sinners

Connect with me:
www.sloanekennedy.com
sloane@sloanekennedy.com

ALSO BY SLOANE KENNEDY

(Note: Not all titles will be available on all retail sites)

The Escort Series

Gabriel's Rule (M/F)

Shane's Fall (M/F)

Logan's Need (M/M)

Barretti Security Series

Loving Vin (M/F)

Redeeming Rafe (M/M)

Saving Ren (M/M/M)

Freeing Zane (M/M)

Finding Series

Finding Home (M/M/M)

Finding Trust (M/M)

Finding Peace (M/M)

Finding Forgiveness (M/M)

Finding Hope (M/M/M)

Love in Eden

Always Mine (M/M)

Choosing Fate (M/F)

Tempting Fate (M/M)

Pelican Bay Series

Locked in Silence (M/M)

Sanctuary Found (M/M)

The Truth Within (M/M)

The Protectors

Absolution (M/M/M)

Salvation (M/M)

Retribution (M/M)

Forsaken (M/M)

Vengeance (M/M/M)

A Protectors Family Christmas

Atonement (M/M)

Revelation (M/M)

Redemption (M/M)

Defiance (M/M)

Unexpected (M/M/M)

Shattered (M/M)

Unbroken (M/M)

Protecting Elliot: A Protectors Novella (M/M)

Discovering Daisy: A Protectors Novella (M/M/F)

Pretend You're Mine: A Protectors Short Story (M/M)

The Four

Forgotten: Luca (M/M)

Foreseen: Lex (M/M)

Forgiven: Con(M/M)

Forbidden: King (M/M)

Non-Series

Watch Me (M/M)

Four Ever (M/M/M/M)

Letting Go (M/F)

<u>**Short Stories**</u>
A Touch of Color
Catching Orion

<u>**Twist of Fate Series (co-writing with Lucy Lennox)**</u>
Lost and Found (M/M)
Safe and Sound (M/M)
Body and Soul (M/M)
Above and Beyond (M/M)

<u>**Crossover Books with Lucy Lennox**</u>
Made Mine: A Protectors/Made Marian Crossover (M/M)

The following titles are available in audiobook format with more on the way:
Locked in Silence
Sanctuary Found
The Truth Within
Absolution
Salvation
Retribution
Logan's Need
Redeeming Rafe
Saving Ren
Freeing Zane
Forsaken
Vengeance
Finding Home
Finding Trust
Finding Peace
Four Ever

Lost and Found

Safe and Sound

Body and Soul

Made Mine

www.ingramcontent.com/pod-product-compliance
Lightning Source LLC
Chambersburg PA
CBHW060933140726
47996CB00001B/475